A PERFECT RHAPSODY

After an unhappy romance with a concert pianist, Emma joins her local orchestra — something she has always wanted to do. Their new young conductor, Paul, seems to be an aloof and arrogant man, but Emma finds herself attracted to him. What secret is he concealing? Will she be able to break through the barrier which he has erected around himself? And how can she ever hope to compete with the beautiful Samantha for his affections, whilst dealing with admirers of her own?

DAWN BRIDGE

A PERFECT RHAPSODY

Complete and Unabridged

LINFORD
Leicester

First published in Great Britain in 2010

First Linford Edition
published 2014

A catalogue record for this book is available
from the British Library.

ISBN 978–1–4448–2078–2

Published by
F. A. Thorpe (Publishing)
Anstey, Leicestershire

Set by Words & Graphics Ltd.
Anstey, Leicestershire
Printed and bound in Great Britain by
T. J. International Ltd., Padstow, Cornwall

This book is printed on acid-free paper

1

'Come in. I'm very pleased to meet you.'

Emma Thornton walked nervously into the room, tentatively grasping the outstretched hand of a tall, distinguished-looking man aged about sixty.

'Sit down and make yourself comfortable,' John ordered, picking up the letter she'd sent applying for a place in the violin section of the Farwell Symphony Orchestra. He perused it while Emma sat watching, wondering why she'd got herself into this situation. She'd never be good enough. She was a mere beginner compared to all the other members. John Grant had been their conductor for many years. He was very fussy about whom he allowed into the orchestra.

'I see you've just passed your grade

six examination,' John remarked. 'Most of our members are grade eight or above. We do achieve a very high standard, so you may find this rather hard.' He rummaged through a pile of music on his desk, carefully selecting one sheet. 'Here, play this for me.'

Emma took it with trembling fingers. She didn't enjoy sight-reading, but knew that with practice she could give a reasonable performance. She rose to her feet, took a deep breath, picked up the violin and started tuning it. *Keep calm. Look carefully at the music. See which key it is in.* She could hear those words in her head. That was what Nick had always said to her. *This is not the time to think of him*, she chided herself. But wasn't it because of him that she was here at this interview?

'Are you ready to start?' John's voice broke into her reverie.

'Yes, I am ready,' Emma replied quickly, pulling herself together. She started playing, hesitantly at first, but then more confidently, realising that the piece was not as difficult as she had feared. She made few mistakes and it sounded quite pleasing even to her ears. When she'd finished she sat waiting while John made notes.

'Well done. That wasn't too bad, was it?' He smiled. 'What have you brought to play to me?'

Emma gave him copies of two violin sonatas. 'Would you like me to accompany you?' he asked.

'Yes please, if you don't mind.'

'I know the keyboard section of this well,' John informed her, indicating one of them, 'so I'll be happy to play the accompaniment.'

'Thank you.' It was Emma's favourite sonata and she soon became engrossed in the music, forgetting her nervousness.

As she ended her recital, John clapped his hands. 'That was lovely. I think you will be good enough for the orchestra. I shall be retiring next month, but a new conductor has been appointed. In fact he should have been here today for your interview, but he must have got held up at work. So in his absence, as we are short of string players, I will take you on.'

Emma beamed. 'Thank you so much. I'm really looking forward to becoming part of the orchestra. I've been to all your recent concerts.' She thought, *I must tell Nick.* Then she remembered that she couldn't tell him anything. He was in New York . . . with Chelsea.

'We'll see you in two weeks for the first rehearsal with our new conductor, Paul Kavanagh. I'll be helping out with the string section then,' John told her. 'Meanwhile, here's some music for you to practise.'

Emma took the sheets from him and was placing them in her bag when John said, 'You say you've been to all our recent concerts. Do you remember Nicholas Brown? He was our solo pianist and he often helped out with the strings. Unfortunately he's gone to America. We really miss him. It's not easy finding good pianists these days.'

'Y . . . yes, I remember him,' Emma murmured. That was her problem. She couldn't forget him.

John shook hands with her once again. Then Emma made her way out of the Farwell Social Centre, where the interview had been held, and walked to the car park. She was strolling towards her Mini when a large impressive-looking black saloon glided to the parking place beside her. She had to move out of the way quickly as the door was flung open and a tall dark-haired man emerged from the interior.

'What do you think you're doing?' she yelled. The tension from the afternoon's activities had built up in her head, and she was feeling fragile and vulnerable. 'You nearly hit me.'

'Of course I didn't. I saw you quite clearly. You almost bumped into me,' the man retorted.

Emma's brown eyes blazed indignantly and her face flushed as she looked up at him. She was tall, but he towered over her. She noticed that he had the bluest eyes she had ever seen. They reminded her of someone she wanted to forget. 'Well, be more careful next time,' she mumbled, unlocking her car. She got in, sensing that he was still watching her.

She started the engine and drove off at top speed, wanting to get home as quickly as possible. She had observed through the rear mirror that the man was continuing to stare after her. *What a supercilious person,* she thought, *even if he is the most attractive man I have ever seen, apart from Nick of course.*

When Emma arrived back at her second-floor flat, she rushed up the stairs, let herself in, and checked her answer phone and mobile to see if there were any messages. As expected, there weren't any. *Nick's not going to get in touch with you again,* she told herself. *It's Chelsea he wants now, not you. Anyway, after what he did, you wouldn't reply even if he had sent you one.*

That evening after dinner Emma

relaxed in front of the television. She couldn't concentrate on the programme and was hardly aware of what it was about. Her mind was full of the day's events and also of Nick. He was the person who would have been most impressed to hear that she'd been taken on by the Farwell Symphony Orchestra, but he'd never know now. He was starting a new life in America with Chelsea.

She thought back over the past two years. Emma had met Nick when she'd been training to teach. He worked in the university music library. She'd gone along to a concert where he was the soloist and had been immediately captivated by the music and the good-looking pianist. A friend introduced them and Emma had said, 'That was brilliant. I love Beethoven and you played it perfectly.'

'Thank you.' Nick smiled. 'I'm glad you enjoyed it, but my playing is far from perfect, I'm afraid.'

'It sounded wonderful to me,' she

replied as she gazed up into his brilliant blue eyes. Soon they were chatting as if they had known each other for years, and when Nick asked Emma to go out with him, she accepted eagerly.

Then she left university and started teaching. She found a flat to rent in Farwell close to her school and to where Nick lived. The two young people began to spend a lot of their spare time together. Emma attended all the concerts that Nick performed in and felt so proud watching him. She was a little disappointed, however, that he hadn't introduced her to the members of the orchestra.

One day Emma confessed to Nick, 'I wish I could play the violin.'

'Why don't you have lessons? I know someone who has a violin to sell and a friend of mine is a very good teacher,' he replied.

A few weeks later Emma was delighted to have her first lesson. She was an apt pupil who practised hard and within two years had achieved grade six. All this time Emma had been dating Nick. She had grown very fond of him and hoped that he felt the same way about her, although he had never actually said he loved her.

At first Nick had helped Emma a lot with her playing and liked to accompany her on the piano, but one day when she asked his advice, he snapped, 'Can't you do anything on your own? I'm not your nursemaid.' Nick quickly apologised when he saw that Emma was upset, explaining that he'd had a bad day at work, but from then onwards she tried not to bother him too much.

Soon after that there was a gala concert at the Farwell Social Centre where Nick was the star performer. Emma sat near the front of the hall, wearing a new peach chiffon dress that she knew flattered her trim figure. As Nick came onto the platform, Emma smiled at him but he looked straight past her and winked at someone who was a few rows behind. Emma turned round and saw a young blonde girl gazing rapturously at Nick. Who was this girl? She'd never seen her before. How did she know Nick?

At the end of the concert, Emma went to meet Nick, but the blonde girl got there first. Emma was aghast to see her throw her arms around him. When Nick saw Emma he quickly disentangled himself from the girl and said, 'Look Chelsea, I have to go now. I'll see you at work on Monday.'

'Who was that?' Emma asked softly, trying to regain her composure, watching as the girl swaggered away.

'Oh, just someone from work. She's here with her father. They come from New York. He's a lecturer over here on a few months' exchange. He arranged for her to have some work experience helping out at our university.'

'You never mentioned her before.'

'I didn't think it was important. She's a nice kid, only eighteen. She'll be going back to America soon.'

Emma said nothing, but thought that

Chelsea didn't look much like a kid.

A few days later Emma went to the university library to meet Nick after work. She arrived early. As she walked in she was dismayed to see Nick at the top of a ladder, putting away some books, while Chelsea was gazing up at him with undisguised admiration. When they were alone, Emma said, 'You do realise that girl's got a crush on you?'

Nick laughed, kissed her forehead and said, 'Don't be so silly. Of course she hasn't.'

Emma continued to feel uneasy. Nick was always busy and she was seeing less of him. She began to suspect that something was going on between him and the young American. Emma kept her thoughts to herself, hoping that it would all blow over when Chelsea went back home. A few days later however, she discovered that her fears had been justified. As Emma walked into the library to meet Nick, she found him with his arms around Chelsea.

'What's going on?' she barked.

'Nothing,' Nick replied as they quickly sprang apart. 'Chelsea was . . . was feeling homesick and I was just . . . just comforting her.'

'She doesn't look very homesick to me,' Emma muttered, noting the smirk on Chelsea's face.

After that, nothing was ever the same between Nick and Emma. He'd tried to assure her that Chelsea was just a work colleague, but Emma felt she couldn't trust him any more.

Then finally everything came to a head one day when she discovered him kissing Chelsea. Emma let out a cry and started to run off.

'Come back. I can explain everything,' Nick protested, catching up with her.

'Leave me alone,' she sobbed, pushing him away. 'We're finished. I don't want to see you again. Go to . . . to your precious Chelsea.'

'If that's what you really want,' he murmured.

'I do,' she whispered.

He turned and walked back to Chelsea, who was waiting with a look of triumph on her face.

Emma was distraught. She went home, threw herself onto her bed and cried until she fell asleep, exhausted. When she eventually calmed down, she decided to concentrate on her violin studies. She'd work hard and become a member of the orchestra. Emma knew they were always looking for new string players. Nick had told her that. She vowed she'd never again allow herself to be taken in by any man. She'd be much more wary in future.

Some weeks after that, Emma received a letter from Nick apologising for upsetting her. He explained that he had fallen in love with Chelsea and was going to America with her. He hoped to find a job in New York and a place with one of the orchestras there. He ended the letter saying, 'I don't think you will be too upset about this, because you've always been like a sister to me.'

Emma had flung the letter down in disgust. She'd fallen in love with him but all she'd been to him was a sister substitute!

*   *   *

Emma switched off the television and got ready for bed. The interview had gone well. She'd achieved her ambition: she was soon going to be a member of an orchestra. A new life was ahead of her. As she tried to sleep, however, the thought that was disconcertingly uppermost in her mind was of the arrogant man with the deep blue eyes, whom she had met briefly in the car park.

*   *   *

The next two weeks passed very quickly. Emma had a lot of work to do to get ready for the new school term. She also practised her violin whenever she could.

Suddenly it was Friday, the day of the

first rehearsal with the Farwell Symphony Orchestra. Emma was excited but nervous, in case she did something wrong. She wondered, too, what the new conductor would be like. She hoped that he would be as kind and considerate as John Grant.

Emma arrived early at the social centre car park. She sat in her car for a while, trying to pluck up courage. When she saw other people going into the hall, she followed behind. To her relief, John spotted her at once and strode over, saying, 'Welcome to the orchestra, Emma. I hope you'll be very happy with us.' He indicated where she should sit, explaining that she would be with the second violins. Then he introduced her to the glamorous middle-aged woman who was sitting next to her. 'This is Anthea. She'll look after you. She knows everything there is to know about the orchestra.'

'Not quite.' The woman smiled. 'I haven't met the new conductor yet.'

'It won't take you long to get to know

him, I should imagine,' John laughed. He turned to Emma. 'If you'll excuse me, I must go and welcome our other newcomer and get myself ready to join the first violins tonight.'

As he walked away, Anthea started chatting about the members of the orchestra and the procedure for the evening. 'Of course, it might all be different now,' she explained. 'None of us have met Paul Kavanagh yet. He's our new conductor. I don't know what he will be like. John is the only one who has seen him, and he was quite impressed, but Paul sounds rather an elusive character to me.'

Emma was beginning to feel more at ease. Anthea was very friendly, as were all the people she'd been introduced to. She tuned her violin carefully and then looked around at her fellow musicians. She recognised several faces from when she'd been in the audience watching Nick performing. There were more women than men, their ages mixed.

The whole orchestra was assembled.

It was time to start rehearsing, but there was no conductor. They gossiped amongst themselves, catching up on their news, as they hadn't met for several weeks due to the summer holiday. John introduced Emma to the other new member, Colin, who was about her own age. He was rather round, with a mop of auburn hair and a friendly, jolly face. He played the viola. Anthea chatted constantly to Emma and Bill, who was seated the other side. Emma noticed that he seemed mesmerised by Anthea, scarcely taking his eyes off her. Emma was amused to see a young couple in the first violin section, holding hands, gazing adoringly at each other, oblivious of everyone else, as were two percussionists. She couldn't help thinking, *This is supposed to be an orchestra, not a marriage bureau.*

Gradually everyone began to get restless. 'Where is he? Where's our conductor, John? What's going on?' a big red-faced man asked.

'Paul must have been delayed. I'm sure he will be here in a minute,' John tried to reassure him.

Suddenly the door at the back of the hall was flung open. *It must be the conductor*, Emma thought. The chatting ceased and everyone turned to watch as someone hurried to the front. Emma tried to look but couldn't see anything because her view was obscured by the large woman sitting in the row behind. As the person reached Emma's row, she looked at his back view. There was something familiar about his appearance, and the way that his dark hair curled around his neck.

There was silence as the very tall man walked up to the stage. He turned round and Emma gasped. *It can't be*, she thought. *I must be imagining things. It can't really be him.*

'Did you say something?' Anthea enquired.

'No, it doesn't matter,' Emma muttered.

The man climbed up the steps onto the dais and Emma saw his face quite clearly. Paul Kavanagh, their new conductor, was the aggressive man she had bumped into in the car park!

2

'Welcome, everybody, to a new year with the Farwell Symphony Orchestra,' Paul Kavanagh was saying. 'I'm very pleased to meet you all.'

Emma couldn't believe her eyes. She felt horrified. Out of all the people in the world, why did this arrogant man have to be the conductor? She'd been looking forward to joining the orchestra for so long, but now she was filled with trepidation. Would he remember bumping into her in the car park? She hoped he wouldn't but feared he might. Then a little voice in her head said, *But didn't you want to see him again? You've thought about that man enough since you first set eyes on him.*

Emma tried to concentrate on what Paul was saying, but instead found herself gazing up at him. *Why does he have to be so attractive? I hope he hasn't seen me.* She moved slightly so that she was shielded by the woman in front. To Emma's dismay, she knocked some music off its stand and it crashed to the floor with a terrible thud. Everyone turned to stare and Colin flashed her a sympathetic smile. Emma blushed and quickly retrieved the music. As she picked it up, she saw Paul frowning. He looked annoyed at some-one interrupting his speech. Suddenly she heard Paul say, 'John has told me that two new members have joined the orchestra, so as it will take me a while to get to know all of you, I'll make a start with them. Would Emma Thorn-ton and Colin Scott please stand up?'

Colin quickly rose to his feet, grinning broadly, but Emma stood up hesitantly, her face flushed.

'I . . . I'm sure I shall remember you two,' Paul stated, looking somewhat startled. 'I . . . I hope you'll both be happy with us.' Everyone smiled and clapped, especially Anthea and Bill.

The orchestra soon settled down to

some serious practice and Emma began to enjoy herself. Anthea kept reassuring her that she was doing well. 'Don't worry about an occasional wrong note. We all make mistakes from time to time. It gets better the more practice you do.'

The time seemed to pass very quickly. Emma had to admit that Paul was an excellent conductor, knowing exactly what he wanted and getting a good response from the players. 'I think we should have a fifteen-minute break,' he told them.

'Come and have a coffee,' Anthea suggested, walking into the kitchen, followed by Bill and several other people.

John Grant came over and asked, 'Is Anthea looking after you, Emma?'

'Yes, very well, thank you.'

'I think you'll find we're a friendly crowd.'

'I'm sure I shall.'

'Don't forget, if you ever need any help or advice, you can always come to me.'

'That's very kind,' Emma replied.

'If you'll excuse me, I need to have a word with Paul.'

As John walked away Colin came up and asked, 'How are you getting on?'

'Fine, thank you. I'm really enjoying it.'

'Me too, but I'm glad I'm not the only new member. It's nice to have someone to compare notes with.'

Emma agreed. She stood chatting to Colin for a few minutes, until a fellow viola player came up, wanting to speak to him. 'I'll see you later,' he called.

As Colin walked away, Emma became aware of a shadow looming over her. She wheeled round quickly, lost her balance and bumped into Paul.

He steadied her and said, 'We meet again, Miss Thornton. You seem to make a habit of bumping into people and things.'

'I'm sorry, Mr. Kavanagh, but I didn't know you were there.' She could feel her face reddening. Why did she have to keep blushing like a schoolgirl? She knew now that Paul had recognised her. She also wondered why she hadn't suspected that the man from the car park was the new conductor.

'I didn't mean to startle you. I just wanted to know if you had enjoyed your first rehearsal with us so far.'

'Yes, thank you. I really like the Grieg piano concerto. Are we going to play that at our first concert?'

'Miss Thornton, you didn't listen to my opening remarks. You must have been too busy fiddling with your music! I told everyone that I'm trying to negotiate getting a soloist. If I'm successful, we will perform it at our concert in November. So we've two months to perfect it. I hope that's perfectly clear. Now please excuse me, I need to sort out something with John.'

Before Emma could think of anything to say in her defence, Paul had moved off. His sarcastic reply had made her feel small and self-conscious. Why did she always get on the wrong footing with him?

Emma tried very hard to concentrate for the second half of the rehearsal and made no more faux pas. At the end as she was gathering up her music, Emma noticed John and Paul talking and laughing together. *He looks stunning when he smiles*, she thought. *The trouble is, I just seem to bring out the worst in him — or is it the other way round?* she wondered. *He brings out the worst in me?*

'Why was Mr. Kavanagh late for the rehearsal?' Emma asked.

Anthea smiled. 'I think you must have been too nervous to take in what Paul said. He did explain it was for personal reasons, but what that means, I've no idea. Anyway, it's time to go home. See you next week.'

Emma watched as Anthea hurried out of the door, followed by Bill, who was chasing after her, saying, 'Wait for me. Wait for me.'

Emma thought, *Poor Bill. Anthea*

can't get away from him fast enough.

Colin waved to Emma and asked, 'Do you need a lift home?'

'No thank you. My Mini's outside.'

They walked to the car park together and stood talking for a few minutes. Paul came past and called, 'Good night.' Then he stopped, turned to Emma and said, 'Miss Thornton, please try not to have any more accidents this week.' Without waiting for a reply, he strode off.

Colin looked bemused and Emma thought, *Ooh that man, he really does annoy me!* She watched as he got into his Mercedes and sped away in a cloud of dust.

★   ★   ★

Emma was very busy the next day, doing housework and making preparations for the new school term. In the afternoon she went into town to do some shopping. She had decided to look round Kavanagh's bookstore. She hadn't been there for some time. Although Farwell was a small country town, it boasted a very fine bookshop, the equal of any in London. People would come from far and wide just to visit it. She had often gone there with Nick to browse. The store also had a good selection of sheet music and Emma had purchased her violin music there. One day Nick had introduced her to the owner, who was a very pleasant man with white curly hair and piercing blue eyes. He and Emma had got on well together and after that whenever he saw her in the store he would come over and talk to her.

What was his name? Emma wondered. It could have been Henry. Or was it Harold? It was something beginning with 'H', she was sure. What did it matter? She hadn't seen him for a long time, not since the day he'd said, 'I wish my sons had met someone like you.'

Emma hadn't realised that he had any children. She'd never seen them in the store. She politely asked, 'What happened to your sons?'

'It's a long story,' he replied, a wistful expression on his face. He didn't elaborate and Emma thought it best to say no more.

It was Hubert. That was what his name was. She'd remembered. This was the first time she'd thought of him since that conversation. She wondered if she would see him that day. Emma made her way to the art department and spent some time browsing there. Then she went to the music section, picked up a manuscript book, paid for it and got on the down escalator. She needed a notebook. That could be purchased on the ground floor.

Emma was so engrossed in her thoughts as she went down that she wasn't aware of the people on the parallel escalator going up. Just before she stepped off, however, she glanced across and to her embarrassment met the gaze of a familiar figure who had started to ascend. She blushed and quickly looked away. *What's Paul Kavanagh doing here?* she thought as she stepped off. What a silly question, she chided herself. *Doing the same as you. Looking at books of course.* She did seem to make a habit of bumping into him though.

After purchasing the notebook, Emma was about to leave the store when she heard the unmistakable tones of Paul's deep voice. 'Miss Thornton, we meet again. I'm beginning to expect to see you wherever I go!'

Emma tried to appear normal, but she could feel her heart thumping at an alarming pace. 'Hello, Mr. Kavanagh. I've been browsing amongst the books. There are so many lovely ones. I wish I could afford to buy some of them,' she gabbled.

'Please call me Paul. Yes, we do have a good stock. I've made sure of that.'

'You? You made sure?' she repeated inanely, gazing into his deep blue eyes.

'Yes. Didn't you realise? I'm the new owner of Kavanagh's bookstore.'

'Oh. I'd no idea.' Emma tried to compose herself. Perhaps she should have known, but she'd never connected his surname with the store.

'It doesn't matter, Miss Thornton.'

'I'm Emma.'

'I do remember.'

'I meant, please call me Emma.'

'Certainly.'

'Er . . . what happened to Hubert? Has he retired?'

'Unfortunately no. He passed away a short time ago. My Dad had a sudden fatal heart attack and I unexpectedly inherited the business.'

'Oh, I'm so sorry. He was such a lovely man, really kind and helpful. You must miss him dreadfully.'

'We do. You knew him well?'

'No, but he often had a chat with me when I came into the store. Everybody liked him.'

'I'm beginning to realise that. I'm finding it hard, trying to live up to his reputation, especially as I didn't expect to inherit the store.'

'You didn't?'

'No. My elder brother should have been the new owner, but things never turn out the way we expect.' His face clouded over.

Emma didn't want to upset him by asking any more questions. She thought he looked distressed enough. She'd seen a different side to Paul. He was no longer the aggressive man, but a more vulnerable human being. She wanted to put her arms around him to comfort him. Suddenly she came to her senses. What was she thinking? Paul was her conductor, and she was just a very junior member of his orchestra. Emma looked away. She'd been gazing at him like a lovesick teenager, and he was staring back at her, waiting for a reply.

'I'm sorry,' she mumbled, her face flushing. 'Life does sometimes play unkind tricks on us.' Now why did she say that?

'That was said with feeling,' Paul replied, looking into her eyes. 'What terrible things have happened to you,

31

Miss Thornton, er . . . Emma?'

Before she could answer, a man tapped Paul on the shoulder. 'I'm sorry to bother you, Mr. Kavanagh, but could you come and have a word with a customer? He insists on speaking to the owner.'

Paul sighed. 'Please excuse me, Emma. We'll have to carry on our conversation another time.' He shook her hand and hurried off after his employee.

Emma went home, her mind in a whirl. She'd only met Paul briefly, but suddenly she couldn't stop herself speculating about him. She also remembered Hubert's remark about wishing his sons had met someone like her. What had he meant? And what had happened to Paul and his brother that caused their father to look so sad that day? Emma wondered, too, what would have happened if one of Paul's employees hadn't interrupted them. However, she consoled herself with the thought that Paul had made a point of following her off the escalator and chatting to her.

★ ★ ★

Emma returned home from the shopping trip to Kavanagh's bookshop, washed her hair, had a leisurely bath and spent time getting her make-up just right. After Nick had finished with her, she'd purchased a new dress to cheer herself up. Emma decided this was the right occasion to wear it. She was going to a barn dance with a friend from school. They'd arranged to meet outside the town hall.

'You look very nice,' her friend Zoe remarked. 'That's a lovely colour. Pink suits you. You're so slim, Emma. I wish I could wear something like that, but I'm too fat. I suppose I should go on a diet, but I like my food too much.'

'You look very nice too,' Emma replied tactfully. 'That's a very pretty top.'

'You really like it? You're not just

saying it to please me?'

'No, Zoe, I mean it. Stop worrying. Now let's go inside.'

It was already crowded in the hall. They sat and watched for a while and then Emma suggested, 'Let's join in the next dance.'

They partnered each other and had great fun together, until Zoe said, 'I'm worn out. Can we have a rest?'

Emma fetched them some drinks and they sat chatting and watching the other dancers. A few minutes later a tall blond man came over to Emma and asked, 'Will you have the next dance with me, please?'

'Er . . . yes, all right . . . that is, if you don't mind, Zoe?'

'No, you go ahead.'

Emma followed the young man onto the floor and the music started up for 'The Waves of Torey.' There were some tricky steps to master, but Emma and her partner soon picked them up. Zoe watched and waved as they went whirling past.

'I'm glad you agreed to dance with me,' he was saying. 'I noticed you as soon as you walked into the hall. I kept wondering how I could get you away from your friend. You seemed to be glued together.'

Emma laughed. 'We've been having fun, learning some of these intricate steps.'

'By the way, my name's Rob and I'm an accountant. I've just moved into the area, so I don't really know anyone yet. I start a new job next week.'

'I'm Emma and I've been living here for two years.'

'Good. Perhaps you could show me around some time? I'm feeling a bit lonely and disorientated.'

Emma hesitated before answering. She didn't want to appear rude, but on the other hand, she had no intention of getting involved with this stranger. 'Tonight is my last fling before going back to school on Monday. You see, I'm a teacher.'

'Even teachers need some time off.

Why don't we have dinner together tomorrow on your last night of freedom? You could show me a good place to eat.'

'I'm sorry, but I'm busy tomorrow.'

'Well, what about next weekend then?'

Emma thought, *He won't take no for an answer. I wish I hadn't agreed to dance with him.*

'What do you say?' Rob persisted.

'Oh, I don't know. I can't think that far ahead.'

Fortunately for Emma, the music stopped then. 'Thank you for the dance Rob. I'll just go and see how Zoe is.' She hurried over to her friend, but he came after her.

'How about the next dance, Emma?'

'I'm too tired.'

'Okay, I'll go and get a drink. I'll see you in a few minutes.'

As he walked away, Emma sighed with relief. 'Thank goodness for that. I thought I'd never get rid of him.'

'Why, what's wrong with him? He

looks all right to me. You have all the luck, Emma. No one's come near me.'

'You can have him.'

'Why?'

'Oh, I don't know. I just don't fancy him. He seems too . . . too pushy.' Then Emma thought, *If Paul Kavanagh was here, you wouldn't refuse to dance with him. But he's not here, and anyway, he wouldn't ask you. He just thinks of you as a silly little girl who keeps bumping into him.*

Emma noticed Rob was heading their way again, so she suggested to Zoe, 'Let's dance.'

When he saw them dancing together, to Emma's relief, he wandered off. It was a long dance with difficult steps to master, which taxed their stamina and brain power, so by the time it was finished they needed another rest. They sat down and Emma jumped when someone tapped her on the shoulder. 'Hello. Am I glad to see you! I looked round and didn't know a soul. Then I felt so relieved when I spotted you, Emma.'

She looked up and was delighted to see Colin. 'Hello. It's nice to see you too. I didn't know you were coming here.'

'I only decided at the last moment.'

Emma turned to her friend, who was looking at them curiously. 'Zoe, this is Colin. He's just joined the Farwell Symphony Orchestra too. And Colin, this is Zoe. We work at the same school. We both teach year three,' she told him.

They shook hands with each other and then Colin said, 'Now the introductions are over, will you dance with me please Emma? You won't mind, will you, Zoe?'

'No, of course not. I'd like to rest a bit longer.'

'Perhaps I could have the one after, with you then?' he suggested to Zoe.

'I'd like that,' she replied.

Colin led Emma onto the dance floor, where they joined other dancers who were all trying hard to follow the instructions of the caller. 'This is great fun,' he remarked after a few minutes. 'I'm so glad I came.'

Suddenly Emma noticed Rob sitting out, staring across at her with a frown on his face. She looked away and concentrated on Colin. 'What made you join Farwell Symphony Orchestra?' she asked him.

'Well, I saw an advert in the paper for string players, and decided to give it a go. I learned to play the viola when I was at school and always enjoyed being in the school orchestra, so I thought it might be nice to do it again. John Grant interviewed me and luckily he took me on. How about you, Emma?'

She was spared from answering as the dance ended. They walked back to where her friend was sitting. Soon he and Zoe were whirling round the room, while Emma sat catching her breath, watching them and thinking how well suited they looked. Both were auburn-haired and a similar height. Zoe was smiling up at Colin and Emma thought she looked quite radiant. They'd make a good couple, she decided.

'How about the next dance?' Emma was startled from her reverie. Rob was standing in front of her.

'Really, I couldn't. I'm too tired.'

'You didn't look very tired when you were with that ginger chap. Who is he?' Rob asked sharply.

'Yes I am tired,' Emma said indignantly, 'And he ... he's a friend. And ... I don't have to ask your permission to dance with him.'

'No, of course you don't. I didn't mean to upset you. I was just being selfish. I wanted you to myself.' Rob knelt on one knee in front of her. 'Sorry, Emma. Please, will you dance with me again? Please say you will, Emma?'

'All right. When this one's finished.' She couldn't help smiling at his antics. He sat beside her and they watched the dancers until the music stopped and Colin and Zoe came back. They were both chatting, Zoe looking very happy.

Emma and Rob walked onto the

dance floor. 'You're the best-looking girl here,' he whispered, pulling her close to him. 'We'll have to do this again some time.'

Emma didn't reply. She was glad that this one was the sort of dance where you kept changing partners. At the end, Rob asked, 'Can I join you and your friends?'

'Of course,' she replied, not wanting to be rude, but glad that Colin was there too. Rob was beginning to make her feel uncomfortable.

The four young people stayed together for the rest of the evening, Rob only leaving her side when he went to fetch some more drinks. When it was time to go home they all walked to the car park together. They reached Zoe's car first and discovered that Colin's was beside it. 'See you on Monday,' she called. 'I'll be in early.'

'So will I,' Emma replied. 'I still need to put some pictures on the walls, and I'm leading the music curriculum meeting, so I'll have to check my files and make sure I've got everything for it.'

'Poor you.' Zoe groaned. 'I hate doing that.'

'You teachers,' Rob grumbled. 'Do you ever stop talking about your work?'

'Not often.' Emma smiled.

Zoe got into her car and Emma wished that hers was not so far away. As if guessing her thoughts, Colin asked, 'Will you be okay finding your car, Emma?'

Before she could reply, Rob answered, 'I'll escort Emma.'

'I'll be all right, thanks. Bye Colin.'

'See you on Friday,' he said as he got into his car.

Emma hurried off with Rob following. As he caught up with her, he asked, 'Why will you be seeing Colin on Friday? I thought you were busy all week.'

'We both belong to the Farwell Symphony Orchestra.'

'How nice,' he said sarcastically. 'Have you thought any more about Saturday?'

'No I haven't. I can't make any more plans at the moment, as I told you.'

'Well I have enjoyed this evening, especially dancing with you, Emma.'

'Good night, Rob.' They reached her car and she put the key in the lock. She felt uneasy and wanted to get away quickly.

Rob stood in front of the door. 'It's early yet, Emma. You don't have to rush off, do you?'

'Yes. I want to go home. Good night, Rob. Can I get into my car please.'

'How about a kiss first?' He put his arms around her.

'Let me go.' She struggled hard to push him away, but he was too strong for her.

'Don't spoil everything, Emma. We had a lovely evening and I know you enjoyed dancing with me. One kiss, that's all I want. Please.'

'No, Rob. Now let me go.'

'Don't be so unfriendly, Emma.' His speech was slurred. 'One kiss won't hurt.' He tightened his grip on her.

'Rob, I think you've had too much to drink. You'll regret this in the morning,' Emma tried to reason with him.

'Why do women like playing hard to get? You want it really. I know you do.' His eyes were glinting menacingly.

Emma was terrified. She would have slapped him if she could, but he held her arms too tightly. 'Stop it, Rob!' she shouted loudly.

Suddenly, to her great relief, someone pushed Rob away and Emma was able to struggle free. She looked up gratefully into Colin's eyes.

3

'Are you okay, Emma?' Colin enquired anxiously as she stood trembling in front of him, her dark curls dishevelled and her handbag open on the ground.

He bent down to retrieve it. As he did so, Rob grabbed hold of Colin, shouting, 'What do you think you're doing? How dare you interfere!'

Trying to defuse the situation, Colin spoke quietly. 'Let go of me, Rob. I think it's time you went home.'

'Don't tell me what to do.' Rob held onto Colin tightly as he endeavoured to get free.

The two men wrestled together as Emma screamed, 'Stop it. Someone will get hurt.'

Colin managed to pull himself away just as Rob's fist hit him hard. He fell backwards, clutching his face in pain, as blood trickled from his nose.

'Now look what you've done.' Emma rushed over to Colin. She rummaged in her handbag, found some tissues and gently wiped his face.

Rob stood staring at them. All the aggression had gone from him. 'I'm so sorry,' he murmured. 'I don't know what came over me.'

'Just go home, Rob,' Colin answered wearily. 'And don't drink so much in future.'

'I didn't mean to hurt you, but I was furious that you came between me and Emma.' Rob looked shamefaced. 'Will you be all right?'

'Yes.' Colin dabbed at the blood, which was still oozing from his nose.

'I think I will go home. I don't feel very well.' Rob turned to Emma. 'I'm sorry. I don't usually behave like this. I'll leave my car here tonight and collect it tomorrow. I think a walk will do me good. I need some fresh air.'

'Good night, Rob.'

Colin and Emma watched as Rob staggered across the car park, lurching

46

from side to side. 'Thanks,' Colin whispered, clutching hold of her hand.

'What for?'

'Tending my wounds.'

'I didn't do much. I think I should be thanking you for rescuing me. I was so glad to see you! I thought you'd probably driven off.'

'I didn't trust Rob, so I sat and waited in my car to make sure you were okay.'

'I'm glad you did. I dread to think what might have happened if you hadn't appeared when you did.' Her voice faltered.

'You're still shaking, Emma.'

'I know. I can't stop. I was really frightened.' Her eyes filled with tears.

'It's all right. You're safe now.'

'Yes, thanks to you.'

Colin put his arm around Emma. She didn't pull away, feeling reassured by his presence. 'I think Rob felt ashamed of himself in the end. Perhaps he'll learn not to drink so much in future.'

'I hope so.'

'I was amazed at how calm you were, Emma, when you wiped the blood from my face.'

'I've been well trained. You have to keep a cool head no matter what happens in the classroom. Anyway, Colin, I think I'd better go home.'

'Will you be able to drive?'

'Yes, I'm fine now. What about you?'

'I'll probably have a black eye in the morning, but otherwise I'm okay. I'll see you to your car then.'

Emma took the key out of her handbag, placed it in the lock and got into her car. Suddenly she heard footsteps coming towards them.

Colin turned round and exclaimed, 'Hello, John, what a surprise. I didn't expect to see you.'

'Oh, it's Colin, isn't it? And isn't that Emma in the car?'

'Yes, that's right.'

Emma wound down the window reluctantly, thinking, *He's going to wonder what's going on.* 'Hello, John.'

48

'Where have you two been?' John asked. Then noticing Colin's nose, which was beginning to swell, he gasped, 'Whatever's happened to you?'

'Let's just say I had a bit of a problem with someone and I came off the worse.'

'Oh dear,' John murmured. 'It looks painful.'

'It is a bit, but Emma was brilliant,' Colin added. 'She's been my nurse.'

Now why did he have to say that? She thought. *John will think we've been out together.*

'We seem to be having an extra meeting of the Farwell Symphony Orchestra in the car park tonight,' John smiled. 'Paul and I were having a drink together when we bumped into Fred, our double bass player. He's having a chat with Paul now. I expect he'll catch us up in a minute. Oh, here he is.'

Emma's heart sank. Paul was the last person she wanted to see at the moment. *Why does he always turn up at the wrong time?* She felt her face flushing and her heart racing.

'Colin, what have you done?' Paul's unmistakeable deep voice boomed out.

He explained about Rob and the barn dance, while Emma was aware that Paul was gazing down at her, his eyes icy like steel. When Colin had finished speaking, Paul remarked, 'So Emma came to your rescue. Aren't you the lucky one?'

She wished that she could become invisible. She closed the window, turned the key in the ignition and called, 'Good night everyone.' Feeling close to tears, she drove straight out of the car park, leaving the others staring after her.

A few minutes later Emma was home. In bed that night her mind was in turmoil. All the events of the evening were churning round and round in her head and sleep was impossible. Was it her fault that Rob had tried to force her into kissing him? Had she led him on? She certainly hadn't meant to. She was grateful to Colin for coming to her aid of course, but she hoped he wouldn't get the wrong impression and think that she was interested in him. Why did Colin have to tell Paul about the barn dance in such detail? *He's the last person I wanted to hear about it. He probably thinks that I went to the dance with Colin.* Then Emma asked herself, *Does it matter? Why would Paul be interested in anything I do?*

Eventually she managed to get a few hours of troubled sleep. In the morning she phoned Zoe and told her what had happened, omitting the part about Paul.

'Oh, that's terrible,' she sympathised. 'I never dreamt Rob would be like that. I do hope Colin will be all right.'

'I'm sure he will,' Emma reassured her friend. 'You liked him, didn't you, Zoe?'

'Yes, he was very nice, but . . . ' She hesitated. 'But he only had eyes for you.'

'Don't be silly. He hardly knows me.'

'What difference does that make? He

likes you, Emma. I'm sure of it.'

Emma quickly changed the subject. That was one complication she didn't want. Colin was just another member of the orchestra, and nothing more. 'I'll have to go now,' Emma told Zoe. 'Still got my planning to do for tomorrow.'

★   ★   ★

During the next few days, Emma was very busy with schoolwork, and getting to know her new class of children. She wasn't able to practise the violin as much as she would have liked.

On Friday she arrived at the social centre car park at the same time as Colin. 'How are you?' she asked, noticing his black eye.

'I'm fine, thanks.'

They started to walk towards the hall, when Emma was alarmed to see Rob appear in front of them, carrying a large bouquet of pink carnations.

'What are you doing here?' Colin growled.

'Don't worry. I've come to apologise. I know I was out of order last Saturday, and my only excuse is that I had too much to drink on an empty stomach, but I've learnt my lesson. It won't happen again. I'll make sure of that.' He turned to Emma. 'Do you think you could forgive me? These flowers are for you, as my way of saying sorry.'

'Thank you, Rob. Let's forget about it.' She took the bouquet from him, feeling embarrassed.

'Perhaps you should cut out drinking altogether if you can't handle it,' Colin advised.

'I'll try. I really will.'

'Goodbye Rob,' Colin said dismissively. 'We'd better go now, otherwise we'll be late. We don't want to give a bad impression at our second rehearsal. Come on, Emma.'

'Can I just put these flowers in my car?' she asked Colin. 'I can't take them into the hall.'

'Okay. I'll come with you, but we'll have to be quick.'

Colin took Emma's arm and guided her away from Rob while he stood watching for a moment, and then walked off.

They had nearly reached Emma's car when Paul Kavanagh strode towards them. 'Oh, hello,' Colin exclaimed, smiling. 'We won't be a minute. Just got to put these in the car.'

Paul looked at Emma clutching the bouquet and then at Colin who was still holding onto her arm. 'Good evening,' he muttered, giving them a hostile glare as he stomped past.

'Not very friendly, is he?' Colin said to Emma. 'I wonder what's up with him.'

'Let's hurry,' was all she could reply, her heart thumping madly and her face scarlet.

When they went into the hall, Anthea spotted Colin's black eye and wanted to know what had happened.

'It's a long story,' he replied. 'Can't tell you now. Got to tune my viola. I'd better find my seat. I'll see you later,' he mouthed to Emma as Paul approached.

A few minutes later the rehearsal started in earnest. Emma began to regret that she hadn't done more practice. Paul was a demanding conductor and she found it hard to keep up.

'Don't worry.' Anthea whispered, sensing that Emma was getting flustered. 'You'll soon get used to it.'

'Stop,' Paul commanded, tapping his baton on the music stand. 'The violinists need to re-tune their instruments.' Emma was sure that he was staring directly at her. There was a loud buzz of sound as John Grant played notes on the piano, while the string players frantically tried to make amends.

'When the leader of the orchestra returns from his holiday, I'll ask him to make sure that you are all ready to start so we don't have to waste valuable rehearsal time as we are doing tonight.' Paul looked aggrieved.

John tried to appease him. 'I'm very

sorry. We're not yet back to our usual routine after the long summer holiday. This won't happen again. Incidentally, the leader's a woman.'

'Sam Johnson. I assumed it was a man.' Paul's face had reddened.

'He doesn't like making mistakes,' Anthea whispered to Emma.

'It's really Samantha,' John replied.

'How was I to know?' Paul snapped.

The rehearsal continued but the atmosphere was charged with tension. Emma was glad when Paul suggested they have a fifteen-minute break. Colin came over and he, Emma, Bill and Anthea went together to get a coffee.

'I think this is going to be a hard year,' Bill remarked. 'I wish John hadn't retired. We had a lot of fun with him. He was always cracking jokes.'

'Yes, that's true, but we've got to give Paul a chance,' Anthea answered. 'After all, it's the first time he's been in charge of an orchestra. He's probably nervous.'

'Nervous!' Bill exclaimed. 'If he's nervous, I'm Father Christmas.'

Anthea and Colin roared with laughter and Emma found herself smiling too.

The second half was no better than the first. Paul was continually stopping, complaining about their technique, timing or phrasing. Emma was beginning to think that she wasn't good enough to be part of the orchestra.

'Don't worry,' Anthea kept reassuring her. 'It'll get easier.'

Emma wasn't so sure.

At the end of the session, Paul said, 'I'm sorry if you think I've been overly critical this evening, but I want us to keep up the high standard that I know you're all capable of. We have a busy year ahead of us with four major concerts, as well as a carol service in Farwell Parish Church, which I hope you will all attend.'

'Good,' an elderly cellist interrupted. 'I take it John will be playing the organ, won't he? He's brilliant.'

'I have heard him,' Paul answered dryly. 'Yes, he will be playing. Now, I hope we all know where we stand. Good night, everyone, and thank you for listening.' There were sighs of relief all round as Paul strode off, accompanied by John.

'I don't think I'm going to enjoy this year,' Bill moaned to Anthea.

'It's too early to say yet. Stop criticising the poor man. He is the boss. It can't be easy for him taking over from John.'

'You women,' Bill snorted. 'Sticking up for him just because he's got a handsome face!'

'Well, you can't deny he's the best-looking man in the room.' Anthea smiled. 'Don't you agree, Emma?'

'Oh . . . er . . . I suppose so,' she murmured, gathering up her music.

'We'll have to see how it goes next week. Good night everyone,' Anthea called as she walked off, closely followed by Bill.

Colin came over to Emma and asked,

'Do you fancy coming to the Farwell Arms for a drink? Several people are going.'

'Don't talk to me about drink,' Emma snapped. 'I haven't got over last Saturday yet.'

'I'm so sorry, Emma. I didn't think.' He patted her hand. 'How about another coffee then?'

She was going to refuse but seeing Colin's disappointed face decided to accept. She didn't want to hurt his feelings. After all, he had come to her rescue the previous Saturday. Talking to him might cheer her up a bit. Emma was feeling quite depressed about the evening. Not only had her performance been inadequate, but also Paul had ignored her.

It was a short walk to the coffee bar. Colin chatted non-stop and she listened. She found some seats while Colin went off to get their drinks. Feeling tired, she rested her chin in her hands and sat thinking about the events of the past few days. Whereas a short time ago her thoughts had been constantly of Nick, now a blue-eyed bad-tempered man occupied her mind instead, someone, who would never be interested in her. He might even be married. Why hadn't that occurred to her before?

'Hello, Emma. I'm sorry I didn't get a chance to speak to you this evening. How are you finding it? I hope we haven't put you off.'

She'd been so wrapped up in her thoughts that she hadn't heard anyone approaching. 'Oh hello, John. No, of course not, but I am finding it a bit hard.'

'You'll soon get used to it. I'll just sit here a minute if you don't mind. I'm feeling rather tired. Must be all that concentrating on playing the right notes.' He smiled. 'I don't have that worry when I'm conducting. I need to find time to do more violin practice.' John sank down into the armchair opposite Emma.

'Me too,' she replied.

'Paul's buying our drinks. Would you like something? You've been staring at that menu for ages.'

'Sorry, I was lost in thought. Colin's gone to get a coffee.'

'Oh, I see.'

What does he see? Emma thought. *Does John think that Colin and I have paired off?*

'Hi, John.' Colin returned carrying two mugs of coffee, and placed them on the table. 'I bought cappuccinos. I hope that was okay, Emma.'

'Lovely, thank you.'

'Can I get you anything, John?' Colin asked.

'No thanks. Paul's getting mine. Here he comes.'

'Come and sit down,' Colin called to Paul. 'There's plenty of room here.'

'Er ... I'd better not ... er ... thanks. There's something I need to discuss with John.'

That's just an excuse, so he doesn't have to sit with us, Emma thought.

'Okay. Good night, you two.' John got

up stiffly and followed Paul across the room.

When they'd gone out of sight, Colin asked, 'Did you see Paul's face? It was like thunder. I was only trying to be friendly. He's so aloof. I wonder if he's ever cheerful.'

'He's probably still annoyed about the rehearsal.' Even now, Emma found herself defending Paul.

'Well, let's hope it's not as bad next week. The only good thing about joining the orchestra so far has been meeting you, Emma.'

She ignored that remark and concentrated on drinking her coffee.

'You're very quiet tonight,' Colin remarked.

'I'm rather tired. It's been a hard week.'

They sat for a few minutes until their drinks were finished, Colin making all the conversation, while Emma gave only brief replies. 'I'd like to go home now,' she said at last.

'I'll walk you to your car.'

As they reached it she sensed that Colin was going to put his arm around her. This was the last thing she wanted, so she dropped her keys on the ground, bent down quickly, picked them up, unlocked the door and got inside, calling, 'Good night, Colin. Thanks for the coffee.'

As she drove off, she could see him staring after her with a puzzled expression on his face.

* * *

During the week Emma practised the violin as much as possible even though she was very busy with schoolwork. She wanted to keep up with the other more experienced players.

At the next rehearsal, everyone was meticulously careful in tuning their instruments. John walked up onto the platform. 'Good evening, ladies and gentlemen. I've had a message from Paul. I'm afraid he's been delayed, so I'm going to take over for now until he arrives.'

They'd just started playing the first piece, when there was a loud crash as the door was flung open and a tall, blonde woman in a cerise tightly fitting dress teetered over to John, who stopped conducting. 'I'm sorry I'm late,' she said to him in a low, seductive voice.

There was a chorus of, 'Hi, Sam. Did you have a good holiday?' Everyone seemed very pleased to see her.

So this is Samantha Johnson, Emma thought. *She's very attractive*.

'Where's our new conductor, John? I'm dying to meet him. What's he like?'

'A bit of a misery if you ask me,' Bill called out.

'Oh, I hope not.' Samantha grimaced. 'We're usually a happy bunch. I'll have to try and soften him up.'

'I think you're the only one who might be able to do that,' Bill smiled.

'That sounds like a challenge I can't resist,' Samantha laughed.

John tapped his baton impatiently on the music stand. 'Now come on everybody, let's get started, otherwise Paul will arrive and we won't have done anything.'

'Okay, John.' Samantha settled down amongst the first violins and the rehearsal proceeded peacefully for the next half-hour.

'Just like old times,' Bill commented.

Emma enjoyed herself. Her extra practice had paid off. She played well and didn't feel intimidated. John was a much calmer and less aggressive conductor than Paul.

It was all going smoothly when Paul walked in. He sat down and watched as John continued to conduct. 'Very good,' he said when the piece was finished.

'Hello, Paul.' John smiled. 'Glad you made it. I'd like you to meet Samantha Johnson, the leader of the orchestra. She's just got back from her holiday.'

Emma watched as Samantha stood up and Paul shook her hand. She couldn't help noticing the appreciative looks he was giving her.

Paul took over and the rehearsal

proceeded smoothly.

During the coffee break, Emma stayed beside Anthea, while Bill went to fetch their drinks. Emma took the opportunity to watch Paul from a safe distance. He and John were talking to Samantha who, although tall, still had to look up to them. She kept touching their arms and was smiling and laughing in a very animated way. Even Paul seemed to have come out of his shell and was joining in with the laughter.

When Bill returned and sat beside Anthea, Colin came over to Emma and remarked, 'You're not avoiding me, are you?'

'No, of course not. Why would I do that? I was just listening to Anthea. She's been telling me about her garden.'

'You're interested in gardening?'

'Well . . . not really, but Anthea is,' Emma whispered, not wanting to offend her.

Colin laughed. 'It's much better this

week, isn't it?' he said, changing the subject. 'Paul's not so grouchy. It must be Samantha who's having a good effect on him. I think he's fallen for her.'

'I'm not surprised,' Bill joined in. 'She is rather dishy and she's available. He's not bad-looking either. They're both in their early thirties, I should think. In fact, they make a handsome couple.'

'He might be married, although he doesn't wear a wedding ring,' Anthea added.

'You don't miss anything,' Bill retorted.

'But you're right, Colin,' Anthea continued. 'Paul's a changed man and it's certainly for the better.'

Emma kept quiet. There was nothing she could say. She wished with all her heart that she didn't find Paul so attractive. She knew that even if he were unattached, there was no hope for her, when someone as glamorous as Samantha was around. *Paul hasn't spoken to me all evening,* she thought. *I don't suppose he will bother with me at all now that she's back. Besides, according to Bill, Samantha is also available, whatever that might mean.*

The rehearsal continued uneventfully. Paul was polite, almost friendly. He made no adverse criticisms and the orchestra played well. Just before they finished, he said, 'I have some good news for you.'

'What is it, Paul?' one of the cellists shouted.

'We have a soloist for Grieg's Piano Concerto. It's someone I think most of you will know. He has agreed to come to our last two rehearsals, so before that John has agreed to stand in as pianist.'

'Good old John,' someone called.

'Who is it, Paul? Don't keep us in suspense.'

'Our soloist will be travelling back from America especially to be with us. It's Nicholas Brown!'

4

Emma dropped her bow on the floor with a loud clatter. Fortunately, no one except Anthea paid any attention. They were all too busy cheering and chatting amongst themselves.

'It'll be lovely to have Nick back again,' Bill enthused. 'He's a very good pianist. Have you heard him, Emma?'

The colour drained from her face as she retrieved the bow. 'Yes,' she murmured.

'Are you feeling all right?' the older woman asked. 'You look very pale.'

Bill also noticed Emma's white face. 'You don't look very well. It's so hot in here. You need some fresh air.'

Emma tried to pull herself together. 'I'm just a bit tired. I'll go home and get an early night for a change.'

'Would you like me to escort you to your car?' Anthea asked.

'No, I'm fine now, thanks.'

Anthea and Bill stood watching, while Emma hurried outside thinking, *Now what can I do? I can't face seeing Nick. Just when I thought I was getting over him, he has to turn up again.* She was so lost in thought that she didn't hear Colin calling.

'Wait for me, Emma.' He caught up with her and tapped her on the shoulder.

Startled, she screamed, 'Oh Colin, you made me jump.'

'Sorry. I didn't mean to frighten you,' he apologised.

'But you did. You shouldn't have touched me.' Then, not wanting to upset him, she said more calmly, 'I'm still in a nervous state after last weekend.'

'I didn't think, Emma. That's my trouble, rushing into things and thinking afterwards.'

'Like when you rescued me and got a black eye for it?'

'Yes, but someone had to do it.'

'And I'm very grateful to you, Colin.'

'How about coming for a coffee with me then?'

'Not tonight, thank you. I really am very tired.' Seeing his crestfallen face, she added, 'Maybe another time.'

'Okay.'

She was about to get into her car, when she groaned, 'Oh no.'

'What's the matter?'

'I've left my music behind.'

'I'll come back with you to get it.'

'I can manage, thanks.'

'I'll come with you,' Colin repeated. 'It's dark and we don't want any more trouble in the car park.'

Emma couldn't argue with that, so they walked back together, meeting Anthea and Bill on the way.

'Is she all right?' Bill enquired.

'Yes, of course she is, she's just forgotten her music,' Colin answered.

'Well, she wasn't a few minutes ago.'

'What's all this?' Colin turned to Emma. 'You didn't tell me anything was wrong.'

'I can speak for myself, you know. I'm perfectly all right.' Her voice was testy. 'I'll collect my music and then I'm going home, so please don't fuss over me.'

Before Colin could say anything else, John Grant appeared. 'I'm glad you've made some friends here, Emma. You can all commiserate together. I know we can be a funny lot at times, but you'll soon get used to us.'

'I'm sure I shall.' Emma tried to smile. 'I've just got to collect my music. I won't be a minute.' She excused herself and hurried into the hall, leaving Colin talking to John.

She picked up the manuscripts and started to walk towards the door when Paul stepped in front of her. 'Hello, Emma. You haven't spoken to me this evening.' He appraised her pale face.

'I could say the same about you, Paul.'

'Well, I have been rather busy.'

Yes, she thought, *chatting up Saman-tha.*

'Emma, I never seem to get a chance to speak to you alone. I . . . I was going to suggest that we finish that . . . that conversation we started in Kavanagh's. Would . . . would . . . you — '

'There you are, Emma.' Colin had come charging into the hall.

Paul grimaced and Emma felt dismayed. It had happened again. He was right. Every time they were together, someone interrupted them. What had he been about to ask?

'Oh, I should have realised that you weren't on your own,' Paul muttered haughtily. It seems that wherever you go, Colin follows along behind. Good night, Emma.'

She watched as Paul strode across the hall, up to Samantha, who gave him a welcoming smile.

'What was all that about?' Colin asked as they went back to the car park.

'Nothing much.'

'He's a strange man. I can't make Paul out,' Colin remarked to Emma.

Neither can I, she thought.

* * *

Emma had a troubled night. *Why is Nick coming back? Will he bring Chelsea with him? How will I cope with seeing him again? Can I stay with the orchestra? What was Paul going to ask? Why does Colin keep turning up at the wrong time?* All these questions kept whirling around in her head and sleep eluded her till dawn.

The next afternoon, Anthea telephoned. 'Are you all right, Emma? You looked so pale last night, I was worried about you.'

'Yes, I'm fine now,' she lied. 'I was just very tired. Had a hard week at school.'

'Why don't you come over for a meal one evening? I'll show you my garden and we could have a good chat.'

'I'd love to,' Emma replied.

* * *

Three days later, Emma made her way to the other side of Farwell. She found

Anthea's bungalow easily. It was the one in the street with the best-kept front garden. After showing her around, Anthea produced a delicious meal. They were sipping their coffee when she said, 'I hope you don't mind me asking, but you used to be Nick Brown's girlfriend, didn't you?'

'Yes.'

'As soon as we were introduced, I knew I'd seen you somewhere before. Then when Paul mentioned Nick and I saw the colour drain from your face, I remembered. What happened to him? Or would you rather not talk about it?'

Suddenly, Emma found herself telling Anthea the whole story.

'I'm surprised at Nick behaving like that,' Anthea remarked at the end.

'Chelsea's so pretty, I suppose Nick couldn't resist her. I couldn't compete with her.'

'Don't defend him, Emma. He doesn't deserve it. I'm sure you're every bit as attractive as Chelsea. You're better off without him.'

'Maybe, but I don't know if I can stay with the orchestra. How can I face seeing him again?'

'Please don't leave. Don't let Nick drive you away. We need you. Besides, Colin would miss you.'

'Colin?' Emma murmured.

'Yes. Anyone can see that he's crazy about you.'

'Oh Anthea, I do want to stay with the orchestra, but I'm not interested in Colin. He's just a friend. That's all.'

'Well, friendship can sometimes lead to something deeper.'

'Not in my case,' Emma stated definitely.

'Okay. I'll say no more. I can understand how you feel. I think of Bill as just a friend too. I know he would like to be more than that, but I'm not interested. I've been married once and that didn't work out. I'm happy living on my own now. I don't want anything to change. Sorry, Emma, going on about my problems. Would you like another coffee?'

'No, thank you. I'd better go now.'

Emma was about to leave, when Anthea said, 'Oh I forgot to tell you. I saw Paul in Kavanagh's Bookstore on Saturday. I hadn't realised before that he was the new owner. It seems his father Hubert died of a heart attack and Paul unexpectedly had to start running it. Did you ever meet Hubert? He was a very nice man.'

'Yes, I did know him.'

'Well, I was going to ask Paul what happened to his older brother . . . Christopher, I think his name was. Haven't seen him for ages. Anyway, I didn't get a chance. Samantha Johnson walked into the store. You should have seen Paul's face. It positively lit up. She seemed equally delighted to see him. I made a quick exit. Samantha's been divorced about six months now. I think she's looking for another romance. I'll be interested to see what happens there.'

★　★　★

At the next rehearsal Paul informed everyone that John had composed a new work especially for the orchestra.

'What's it called?' Bill asked.

'The Farwell Rhapsody,' Paul replied. 'I'll be handing out copies to each of you as soon as they come from the printers.'

'Well done, John,' Bill shouted, and they all clapped and cheered.

'We've performed quite a few of his pieces over the years,' Anthea whispered to Emma. 'He's very clever.'

During the coffee break, Emma observed Paul talking to Samantha, who was looking ravishing in a tightly fitted red dress. After a few minutes Colin came over to chat to Emma, Anthea and Bill.

Bill suddenly remarked, 'Look at Paul and Sam. They can't take their eyes off each other. I told you they'd have a romance.'

'I told you, Bill,' Anthea stated.

'Don't argue about it,' Colin laughed, winking at Emma. 'We can all see what's going on there, can't we? The good thing is that since Samantha's been around, Paul's been in a much better mood.'

'Yes, but he is a bit of a mystery man. We still don't know much about him,' Bill added.

★　★　★

The following Monday morning, Emma got up early, practised her violin before breakfast and was about to leave for school when the postman arrived. She picked up a handful of letters, perusing them quickly. Then her heart felt as if it had missed a beat. One of them had an American stamp. *No, not him! It can't be. He wouldn't write to me again, would he?* She turned the envelope over and on the back was the name of the sender, Nicholas Brown.

Emma put the mail on the table and hurried off to school. All day long she kept wondering why Nick had written to her. Just when she was getting over him, he had to open up old wounds.

When she arrived home that evening, Emma made her evening meal and sat staring at the letter. *Should I open it or throw it away?* she wondered. Finally she decided it would be best to find out what it contained. *After all, I have to see Nick again in a few weeks. At least I know that I'm not in love with him any more, but I do remember the anguish he gave me. It's someone else who's causing me pain now. Why do I always fall for the wrong man? Perhaps if Samantha Johnson hadn't been in the orchestra, Paul might have noticed me. He was quite friendly that day I met him in Kavanagh's and he did say that he wanted to continue our conversation. Now I've no chance though. Sam's so glamorous. Stop wallowing in self-pity*, she urged herself.

Emma's fingers trembled as she tore open the letter. She became more and more angry as she read it. *How dare he? He's got some cheek*, she thought, tearing it into tiny pieces. *I'm not replying to that*. If only he wasn't coming back to Farwell as their soloist!

Emma stomped around her flat, unable to settle to anything. She tried ringing her parents for a chat but there was no reply. *I suppose they're out enjoying themselves*, she thought enviously.

After a miserable evening, Emma felt worse in the morning. Her head was aching and she didn't feel like facing her class of children. Somehow she made it through the day. Her class seemed particularly noisy and she'd had to raise her voice several times in order to be heard. By then her throat was very sore. *Serves you right for shouting at the children*, she chided.

Emma was on her way home when she remembered that she needed to purchase a birthday present for her father. She went into Kavanagh's Bookstore, selected a couple of detective novels which she thought her father would like, paid for them at the till and was just about to make her way to the exit when she saw Paul standing by the staircase. Although he had his back to her, she recognised him by his arrogant stance, and the way his hair curled around the nape of his neck. He was not alone, however. Samantha, in a tight-fitting jade suit, was holding onto his arm, smiling up at him. Emma could hear his resonant voice. Her eyes pricked with tears as she took in the scene. *Sam's so gorgeous*, she thought. How could Paul not find her irresistible?

Emma wanted to get away quickly, unnoticed, but was embarrassed when she couldn't stop herself from giving a loud sneeze. She slunk out of the shop and then quickened her pace. Suddenly she became aware of footsteps behind her and a deep voice calling out, 'Emma, don't run away. Wait for me.'

She turned around and looked straight into Paul's eyes. 'Oh, hello. I didn't see you,' she lied.

'I hope you found what you were looking for in the store,' he said.

'Yes, thank you. I bought a couple of books for my dad.'

'You sound out of breath,' Paul remarked, looking at Emma intently. 'I'd been talking to Samantha Johnson when she noticed you. I called out, but you didn't hear, so I excused myself from Sam and came running after you. You seem in rather a hurry. Are you meeting someone? Not Colin, is it?'

'No. I'm not meeting Colin or anyone else,' Emma snapped. 'I was just on my way home from school.' She gave another loud sneeze. 'I've had a hard day.'

'Caught a cold, have you?'

'I think I must have.' Emma's voice was hoarse.

'Whenever I meet you, I expect to see Colin or some other man following along behind.'

'I don't spend all my time with Colin,' Emma retorted indignantly. 'I only see him at rehearsals.'

'And barn dances,' Paul interrupted.

'He just turned up there. I didn't

know he was going. Anyway, I don't have to justify myself to you.'

'No, you don't.'

'That's right. I can do what I like, so I'm going home now.'

'But I was hoping we could continue our conversation. You know, the one we started when I met you on the escalator, or have you forgotten? But if you're not feeling well, we'll have to leave it again.'

'Of course I remember our conversation. I've just got a cold. There's nothing wrong with my memory,' Emma retaliated, at the same time elatedly thinking, *Paul left Samantha to speak to me!*

'Can we talk?'

'Whenever we do, you keep making remarks about Colin. I can't think why.'

'Can't you, Emma?'

'No. Look, I'd better go now.' She turned away, but Paul caught hold of her arm.

'Don't get angry with me,' he pleaded. 'Can't we start again?'

'Start what?' The words came out before she could stop them.

Paul looked startled, but answered, 'Emma . . . I . . . I would like it if you would have dinner with me tomorrow evening or whenever it suits you.'

She stared at him, stupefied. This was the last thing she had expected. *He must be interested in you*, she thought, *and he can't be married. But what about Samantha? Everyone thinks they're having a romance.*

'Have you nothing to say, Emma?' Paul was waiting for her reply. 'Would it be so terrible to have dinner with me?'

'Oh . . . I . . . I'm sorry. You just took me by surprise.'

'Well, will you come with me, or are you seeing Colin instead?'

'No, Paul. I am not going anywhere with Colin, as I've already told you, and even if I was it's none of your business. He's just . . . a . . . friend.'

'I think Colin sees you as more than a friend, but you haven't answered my question. Will you have dinner with me?

If you're expecting me to go down on one knee, you're unlucky.' He sounded exasperated.

Why don't you just say yes? You want to go out with Paul. Why do you keep arguing with him all the time? To her annoyance she found herself saying, 'You seem to have such a bad opinion of me, I can't imagine why you would want to have dinner with me.'

'For a teacher, you seem to lack imagination.'

'How do you know I'm a teacher?'

'John told me. What makes you think I have a low opinion of you?'

Paul was still holding onto her arm. She disentangled herself, faced him and murmured, 'You think I'm not very good at playing the violin.'

'I've never said that.'

'You didn't need to. I saw the look on your face at the rehearsal.'

'What look?'

'Oh, it doesn't matter. Forget it.'

'Tell me what look I'm supposed to have given,' Paul insisted, glaring at her.

'You're doing it now.'

'I'm just waiting for your answer. Oh Emma, you're the most infuriating person I've ever met.'

'Why bother with me then?'

'And why do you turn everything into an argument? Listen Emma, I . . . I . . . I'd like . . . to . . . get to know you better.' Paul smiled. 'And as your conductor, it's my duty to find out about you.'

'Duty? So that's why you're asking me out? No thanks,' she snapped.

'What are you so upset about?' Paul frowned.

'I assume you're inviting all the other female members of the orchestra out for dinner too.'

'No, of course not.'

'Shouldn't you get to know them too? Or is it just me you want to find out about, because you think John made a mistake in taking me on?'

'Stop jumping to the wrong conclusions.' His voice was edgy. 'I can't imagine what you're getting in a state about, Emma. I was joking when I said it was my duty to get to know you. Surely you realised that?'

'Well I didn't think it was very funny.'

'I'm sorry if you don't understand my sense of humour, and I don't know why you are so insecure about being in the orchestra. If John chose you, that's good enough for me. I respect his judgement. There. Does that make you feel better?'

Emma groaned, 'You're so sarcastic.'

'Maybe, but you're acting like a coy schoolgirl. For the last time, will you have dinner with me?'

'No, Paul. It wouldn't work,' she hissed. 'Go back to Samantha.' *Why am I saying this?* Emma thought. *I don't want him to go to Samantha. I want Paul myself. It's my stubborn pride that's spoiling everything.*

'What do you mean?' Paul shouted.

'I'm sure you don't think she's a coy schoolgirl.'

'My opinion of Samantha is nothing to do with you,' Paul answered sharply.

'And what I think of Colin is no concern of yours either.'

'Point taken. Samantha is a very fine violinist and a good leader of the orchestra and she also shares a similar sense of humour.' Paul's eyes flashed. 'So you won't have dinner with me?'

'No. You're so conceited. You find it hard to believe that anyone could reject you. Go to Samantha. She'll laugh at your jokes. She'll have dinner with you.'

'If that's what you want, Emma.' Paul's face was red but his voice was icy. 'I think I will. At least she acts her age.'

'Just go, Paul.' Emma was close to tears. She turned and ran, leaving him staring after her. All the way home, she was wondering why she'd acted in such a stupid way and messed everything up. *Now you've thrown Paul and Samantha together, and lost any opportunity you ever had with him.*

5

Emma decided to have an early night. She had a pile of marking to do, so she sat up in bed with a mug of coffee trying to concentrate on reading all the stories which her class had written, but her mind was not on it. Instead she found herself mulling over the argument she'd had with Paul, bitterly regretting her actions. Why had she been so hasty? Surely the most significant fact was that Paul had invited her out, not Samantha. She should have accepted, instead of worrying about his motives. Maybe she had misjudged him. She would have to apologise, but would he accept? She'd try on Friday at the next rehearsal, if she got the chance. Why did Paul have this drastic effect, making her act completely out of character? She'd never behaved like this with anyone else.

Emma was startled by her mobile phone ringing. It was Zoe. 'I just wondered how you were,' she said. 'You didn't seem to be your usual self at school today. I won't see you tomorrow. I'm on that I.T. course.'

'I'm okay, thanks. Just got a cold coming on and . . . and . . . '

'And what?'

'I had a letter from Nick.'

'Oh Emma. What did he want?'

'He's coming back to England to be the soloist with the orchestra and . . . and . . . he . . . he's finished with Chelsea.'

'I thought she was the love of his life. He doesn't want you to go back with him, does he?'

'That's what he said.'

'Oh no Emma, you wouldn't, would you?'

'No. Never.'

'Good. He's not worth it, the way he treated you. What else did he say?'

'He's sorry for what he did and

hopes I'll forgive him. He says he's grown up a lot and knows that it's me he wants, not Chelsea.'

'What's happened to her?'

'I don't know.'

'Is Nick coming back to England to live?'

'No. He'll just be here for a few days before the concert, but he's invited me to stay with him in America for Christmas. Can you believe it?'

'After what he did?'

'Exactly. I'm so furious. I wish I didn't have to see him again. He's such a talented pianist, though. I think all the adulation has gone to his head.'

'It sounds like it.'

'Nick's so conceited. It hasn't occurred to him that any woman could resist his charms.'

'Have you answered his letter?'

'No. I've torn it to shreds. I'm not going to reply.'

'Good for you, but he'll get a shock.'

'Probably. I think I'd better stop talking, Zoe. My throat is so sore.'

'You do sound croaky. Bye Emma. Hope you feel better soon.'

That night she found it hard to sleep. She kept thinking about her conversation with Paul and the letter from Nick. She knew what she was going to do about him, but had no idea if she could do anything to resolve her problems with Paul. Why did she have to find him so irresistible? Was it because there was an aura of mystery surrounding him? She knew so little about him. Why did he inherit Kavanagh's Bookstore instead of his elder brother? What happened to his brother? Why had Paul never married, or had he? *If I'd agreed to have dinner with him, I'd probably have found out the answers. Why am I so stupid? The man of my dreams asks me out and I refuse because of some silly argument, which I started. If I do manage to apologise on Friday, will he accept it? If he does, will I be brave enough to ask him if his offer of dinner is still on?*

*   *   *

93

On Wednesday morning, Emma's cold was much worse. She struggled through the day at school and by the time she arrived home she was very hoarse. The next day she could scarcely speak at all. She regretfully telephoned her school to say that she wouldn't be able to come in. Emma felt dreadful about this as she knew the chaos it caused when a teacher was absent, especially at this time of year when they'd all be busy practising for the Harvest Festival. To her relief, the head teacher was very kind and understanding and told her not to worry.

Emma stayed in bed on Friday, determined that she'd get herself fit to go back to school on Monday. She was upset at missing the rehearsal in the evening and also her opportunity to apologise to Paul. She wondered if he had noticed that she wasn't there. He might even think she'd stayed away because of the row they'd had. She guessed Samantha would be giving him her undivided attention. This thought did not cheer her up.

On Saturday morning the telephone rang. Emma crawled out of bed, sank down into her comfortable armchair and croaked, 'Hello.'

It was Anthea. 'I can tell by your voice why you weren't at the rehearsal last night. You sound terrible.'

'I was really sorry to miss it. I expect I caught this cold from one of the children in my class.'

'We had quite a good evening, actually. There were no complaints about our playing from Paul.'

'That was because I wasn't there,' Emma muttered.

'Don't be silly. You're doing very well. The reason why I rang you up, apart from finding out how you were, was to warn you that Colin will be coming round to see you.'

'Oh no,' Emma groaned.

'Paul gave out another sheet of music,' Anthea continued. 'I offered to bring yours round, but Paul said he would do it. Then Colin came up and told him that wouldn't be necessary. He would bring it himself, and save Paul the bother, as he had something he wanted to ask you. You should have seen Paul's face. It was black as thunder. I don't think he likes Colin very much.'

'Oh Anthea, I'm really not in the mood to see Colin.'

'I knew you wouldn't be, but I couldn't do anything to stop him.'

'It's not your fault. I suppose he's only trying to be helpful.'

'You could say that, but I think Colin just wants any excuse to see you. Anyway, a few minutes later, Samantha arrived. She'd had to work overtime. During the break, she made a beeline for Paul. The two of them spent the whole time laughing and joking together. He seemed much more cheerful after that. Samantha's been without a man for a few months now, so she's obviously wasting no time in trying to hook Paul. Are you still there, Emma? You're very quiet.'

'Yes, I'm still here, but I can't talk much.'

'Sorry, I forgot. Well, as I was saying, Samantha's out to get Paul and by the looks of him last night, he doesn't mind at all.'

'Did Colin say when he was coming?' Emma asked changing the subject.

'Some time today, I think.'

'I'd better get dressed then.'

'I had to give Colin your address. I hope you don't mind.'

'No, that's all right, you had no choice.'

After she'd hung up, Emma thought, *If Colin hadn't interfered, Paul would have come round here, and then I could have apologised to him. Now it's too late. Samantha's got her claws into Paul and she won't let go until she's got him, according to Anthea.*

Emma had a warm bath, dressed in a simple blue shift and applied some make-up to her pale face. Although she felt a little better, she was not looking forward to seeing Colin. What was he going to ask? *I hope he doesn't want me to go out with him. He's nice enough and he means well, and I don't want to be rude, but I've no intention of getting involved with Colin.*

Later that afternoon, he arrived at Emma's flat. He was carrying a bouquet of chrysanthemums. 'I hope these will cheer you up,' Colin said, thrusting them into her hands. 'I guessed you must be ill when you didn't turn up for the rehearsal last night.

'Thank you. They're beautiful.'

'How are you?'

'Getting better. It was just a cold.'

'What a lovely flat,' Colin remarked, gazing around. 'And you have so many books.'

'Well, I enjoy reading.'

'Like me. I think we've got a lot in common, Emma.'

'I won't be a minute. I'll put these in water. Sit down and make yourself comfortable,' she replied, walking into the kitchen. 'Would you like a coffee or a cup of tea?' Emma felt she had to be hospitable.

'Coffee please, if it's not too much trouble. I'll make it for us, if you're not up to it.'

'No, I'll do it. I won't be long.'

When she returned to the lounge a few minutes later carrying their drinks, Colin was studying the pictures on her wall. 'These are very good. Who painted them?'

'My brother.'

'He's talented too, like his sister.'

'Anthea said you had some music for me.' Emma ignored his remark.

'Yes that's right. Our illustrious conductor was going to bring it round, but I told him not to bother, as I wanted to see you. Anyway, I knew that he'd be busy with Samantha. She seems to have really fallen for Paul. She couldn't keep her hands off him last night. I've noticed that there seem to be quite a few romances going on amongst the members of the orchestra. Paul and Samantha, Anthea and Bill, and of course, you and me, Emma,' he added shyly. 'You know I'm beginning to fall for you, Emma. I think we make a good team.' Colin took hold of her hand. 'There's something I want to ask.'

She pulled away quickly. 'I think I heard my mobile. It's in the kitchen. I won't be a minute.' Emma hurried out of the room, closing the door behind her. What was Colin going to ask? *He's certainly got the wrong idea about us. I hope I haven't led him on. I didn't mean to. I'll have to let him down gently. If only Paul had come round with the music, this tricky situation could have been avoided and I might have been able to apologise to him. It seems that Colin is continually coming between Paul and me.*

Emma took a deep breath, walked back into the lounge and sat down facing Colin.

'I've been invited to a wedding,' he told her. 'An old school chum's getting married in October. He's said that I can bring a friend, and I ... I ... was wondering if you . . . you would come with me. That was what I wanted to ask. He's a great guy, and . . . '

'What date is it?' Emma interrupted.

'October the twenty-fifth.'

She heaved a sigh of relief. So that was what he wanted to ask. She'd begun to think it was something much more serious. 'Oh . . . it's . . . it's my half term holiday then and . . . and . . . I'll be going to stay with my family for a few days.' *That's got me out of a tricky situation*, she thought.

'What a shame!' He looked crest-fallen.

'I am sorry, Colin.'

He took hold of her hand again. 'Never mind. There'll be plenty of other things for us to do together. What about next Saturday? If you're better of course, we could . . . maybe . . . have dinner together?'

'No.' Emma plucked up her courage. She had to do it. 'I'm sorry, but there's no easy way to say this, Colin.'

'What do you mean?'

'Please don't be hurt, but there's no romance between us. You're a good friend and I'm glad we both joined the orchestra at the same time, but that's all.'

'So, you don't fancy me?'

'I like you Colin, but — '

'Well, that's good enough for me,' he interrupted. 'You've said you like me. Love can grow from that. I'm prepared to wait. I shouldn't have talked about romance. It was too soon. We'll leave things as they are, and see what happens. What do you say, Emma?'

'I don't want to give you false hopes.'

'You haven't. It's early days yet. Anything can happen.'

'But Colin, nothing ever will.'

'What do you mean?' he asked dejectedly. 'Are you telling me there's someone else?'

'Er . . . yes . . . er, I don't know.'

'Who is it?'

'There is no one else,' she lied. 'You're getting me confused. I don't mean to be rude, Colin, but even if there was, it's really none of your business.'

'Sorry, Emma. I'll say no more now, but just remember, if you ever change your mind, I'll be waiting for you.'

'I'm sorry but I won't.'

'I'll leave you in peace then. Good night, Emma. I hope you'll soon feel better.' Colin let himself out, walking ponderously, his face gloomy, his natural air of cheerfulness gone.

Emma felt terrible for upsetting him, but knew she'd had to do it.

★ ★ ★

That evening she had a call on her mobile from her brother Ben, telling her about his latest girlfriend and their exploits. Emma couldn't help feeling a little jealous. Everything seemed to go smoothly for other people, but her life was always complicated. She'd hardly finished speaking when the telephone rang. She picked up the receiver, wondering who it could be. 'Hello,' she said breathlessly.

'How are you, Emma?'

Her heart missed a beat when she heard Paul's serious voice. 'I . . . I wasn't expecting you to ring,' she replied hoarsely.

'I bet you weren't, after the lambasting you gave me on Tuesday.'

Now's my chance to apologise, Emma thought. *I mustn't mess it up this time.* 'I'm very sorry, Paul. I don't know what came over me. I don't usually behave like that.'

'I should hope not. I'll put it down to your cold, shall I? You haven't answered my question. Are you feeling better?'

'A little, thank you.'

'We missed you last night, especially Colin. He was like a fish out of water.'

'Don't go on about Colin again.'

Ignoring her reply, Paul continued, 'I intended bringing round some new music for you, but Colin said he'd do it as he needed to see you.'

'Yes thank you, he's given me the music.'

'So, he's been to your flat. What is going on between you?' Paul exploded.

'Nothing.'

'You told me you were just friends.'

'We are. Why won't you believe me? Anyway, what about you and Samantha?' The words were out before she could stop them.

'Samantha? What's she got to do with anything?'

'Oh Paul, everyone knows about you and Sam. You're always together.' *I'm doing it again*, she thought, *arguing with Paul*.

'How dare you!' he shouted. 'What I do with Sam is my business.'

'And what I do with Colin is mine.' Then more calmly she added, 'I shouldn't have said that about Sam.'

'No, you shouldn't.'

'But when you keep mentioning Colin, I get so annoyed I have to strike back.'

'I thought that was what red-heads did, but you're a brunette.'

In spite of herself, Emma had to

smile. 'Okay Paul, let's have a truce. I'll keep quiet about Samantha, if you do about Colin.'

'All right.'

'Paul . . . ' Emma hesitated.

'Yes.'

'Is the offer still on?'

'What offer?'

'You're determined to make me eat humble pie,' she moaned. 'You know what I'm talking about.'

'I do?'

'Yes, you're enjoying this.'

'Am I?'

'Oh Paul, you're so exasperating!' Emma shrieked.

'And you're not?'

'All right, you win.' She plucked up her courage. 'Paul, if the offer is still on, I'll have dinner with you, when this cold's gone.' *I've actually asked him to go out with me, she thought. Whatever's come over me? I've never acted like this before. It's gone very quiet. He's shocked. I shouldn't have asked. He is going out with Samantha.*

'Are you there?'

It seemed an age before Paul replied, 'Yes I'm still here.'

He's avoiding giving an answer. He's paying me back. It's all my own fault.

'Yes, Emma, I'll take you out to dinner next Saturday. Does that suit you?'

'Thank you, Paul. That will be lovely.' She tried to speak calmly, but inside she was feeling elated.

'We'll arrange it next Friday. Meanwhile, you get better. I'll see you then. Good night, Emma.'

She hung up in a daze. So Paul had forgiven her. She'd have to make sure she didn't upset him again. He couldn't be interested in Samantha then, unless he was taking her out as well. Surely he wouldn't do that, would he?

* * *

On Thursday evening, Emma received a telephone call from her mother, who sounded distraught. 'I'm sorry to tell you this dear, but your gran has had a stroke.'

'Oh no. Is she very bad?'

'We're not sure yet. The doctors are doing tests. She's conscious and talking though, so that's a good sign.'

'Yes, she's quite tough. I've never known her to be ill. Even after Granddad died, she seemed to cope well.'

'You're right. She's a strong woman. We'll all have to hope for the best. Anyway, I was wondering if you could come and see her on Saturday. I know it would cheer her up.'

'Yes, of course I'll come.'

They made arrangements for Emma to stay with her parents for the weekend. As soon as she'd finished speaking, she started making plans. *It's a good thing my cold's better, otherwise I wouldn't be able to visit Gran. I do hope she'll get over the stroke. I'll have to miss the rehearsal again on Friday and my dinner date with Paul on Saturday. Still, it can't be helped.*

I'll have to ring him and explain everything. I'm sure he'll understand. We'll have to arrange some other date to have dinner. I wonder if we ever will go out together.

Later that night, Emma dialled Paul's number. After a few seconds she heard a woman's voice saying, 'Hello, can I help you?'

6

'Hello,' the woman repeated. 'Can I help you?'

'I . . . I want to speak to Paul Kavanagh,' Emma replied hesitantly, 'but I may have the wrong number.'

'No, this is his house. I'm sorry, he's not here at the moment. Can I take a message?'

'I . . . I'm Emma Thornton, a member of his orchestra.'

'Oh hello, Emma. Paul had to go out suddenly. The burglar alarm went off at the store. It's probably nothing, but he had to go and check. I don't know what time he'll be back, but I'll let him know you rang.'

'Thank you. Could you please tell him that I won't be at the rehearsal tomorrow, as my grandmother's had a stroke and I'll be away for the weekend visiting her.' Emma wanted to say she wouldn't be able to see Paul on Saturday either, but thought it best not to mention that. After all, she had no idea to whom she was speaking.

'I'm sorry to hear that,' the woman replied. 'Don't worry, I'll give him your message.'

Emma hung up feeling bemused. So Paul doesn't live on his own. Who was that? *He can't be married. He wouldn't ask me to go out with him if he was, would he?* Could it have been a housekeeper? *Do people still have them?* Emma wondered. Nobody she knew did. At least it wasn't Samantha. This woman's voice was nothing like hers. But then, people often sounded different on the telephone. No, it wasn't Samantha. She was sure of it. So, who was it? Was it his girlfriend? She didn't sound very young, but Emma guessed that Paul was quite a few years older than her. He was maybe thirty-five or thirty-six. It couldn't have been his mother, could it? Men of that age didn't usually live at home with their parents, but his father had died so it was possible that he had returned to keep his mother company. Emma realised then how little she knew about Paul, even though he was constantly on her mind.

★ ★ ★

The weekend passed quickly. Emma's parents were very pleased to see her. Her brother, too, made a fleeting visit. She enjoyed spending time with them all and they were delighted when the doctor told them that Gran was making excellent progress and with physio-therapy would most likely completely recover from the stroke.

Emma arrived back at her flat on Sunday evening. She was getting ready for bed when suddenly the smoke alarm went off. Her first thought was that there must be something wrong with it, but to her horror, she realised that other alarms were sounding too, and she could detect a faint smell of smoke.

She quickly looked around to reassure herself that it wasn't coming from inside her flat. Then instinct told her to get out; there was a fire in one of the other flats.

She put on a jacket and hurried onto the landing, where the residents were gathered. They were anxiously looking at the end flat, where they could see smoke billowing from under the front door. The next-door neighbour was banging on it and shouting.

'No one's in there. They're away on holiday,' someone called. 'They'll be back tomorrow. I've called the fire brigade. They should be here soon.'

'What a shock for that poor family,' an elderly lady sighed.

'We'd better all go down into the car park, away from the smoke and clear of the windows in case the glass blows out,' a young man who'd taken charge of the situation ordered. 'There's nothing we can do up here. We'll leave it to the experts. Let's hope it doesn't spread. I've made sure everyone's out of the other flats. Let's go down. Don't anyone try to use the lifts.'

A subdued, worried group of individuals hurried to the car park. Some had obviously been asleep or getting ready for bed, and had donned dressing gowns. Others were in raincoats and a few were in their indoor clothes, although it was a cold early October night. All were gazing incredulously up at the burning flat.

'Whatever started it?' someone asked. 'Could it have been deliberate?'

'I've no idea,' the young man replied. 'It's no use speculating. Let the fire brigade sort it out.'

Emma was listening to all this as if in a dream, when the sound of the fire engine's siren was heard.

The young man rushed over to the fire fighters and gave them the necessary information as they sprang into action.

'We'll have to break the door down,' he was told.

This was done and the blaze was

quickly brought under control. One of the firemen commended the young man for his prompt actions, in making sure that all the other residents were safe. It was thought that the fire had been caused by an electrical fault in an overloaded and unprotected airing cupboard. The landlord had arrived on the scene by this time and told everyone that he would personally make sure that the wiring in every flat was checked. Emma was glad that hers had been done before she moved in. Her father had insisted on this.

'It's lucky that no one was in the flat at the time,' Emma's neighbour remarked, and everyone agreed whole-heartedly.

When it was safe to return to her flat, Emma was no longer tired. All the events of the past few days were churning in her head. Thoughts of the fire as well as her grandmother, Nick, Colin, Rob, Samantha, Paul and the woman who answered the telephone were filling her mind. She put on her dressing gown, made a milky drink, selected a CD of soothing music, and settled herself down on the sofa with a magazine to try and relax for a while before going to bed. She was startled when the doorbell rang, but hurried to answer it, thinking it was one of her neighbours with further information on the fire.

To her surprise, it was Colin. 'I had to make sure you were all right,' he said, looking at her anxiously. 'I heard there'd been a fire at Farwell Court. I immediately thought of you. What happened, Emma?'

'I'm not too bad, thank you. Just a bit traumatised, I suppose. Still in a state of shock really. You'd better come in for a minute, though. It's too cold to stand talking on the doorstep.' She pulled the belt on her dressing gown tighter.

'Sorry, Emma. I don't want you to catch another cold. You've hardly had time to get over the last one.' He followed her inside and sat down.

'Would you like a coffee?' she asked.

'No, thank you. I don't want to put you to any bother.'

'It's no bother.'

'No, I'm fine.'

'How did you find out about the fire?'

'I was out having a drink with a friend when someone came into the pub and said there was a fire at Farwell Court. I was so worried, I had to come over here to see if I could be of any help.'

'That was very kind of you, Colin. I keep thinking of the owners of the flat. It's terrible. All their possessions were destroyed.' Emma shuddered.

'I'm so glad you're all right. What exactly happened?'

She told Colin everything she knew and he listened intently, a look of concern etched on his face. Emma found herself shaking as she recounted the evening's events.

'You poor thing. You're trembling,' Colin exclaimed, taking hold of her hands. 'You've had a bad time recently

— catching that cold, your grand-mother having a stroke, and now the fire. 'Are you sure your wiring's safe?' he asked.

'Yes. My dad made me have mine checked before I moved in.' Emma pulled her hands away and clasped her mug of coffee.

'Good. That's a relief. How is your gran? I was very sorry to hear about her.'

'We think she'll make a complete recovery, thanks.'

'We missed you on Friday. The funny thing was, though, that Paul seemed to know already. When I arrived, Anthea and John were talking and she told me about your grandmother.'

'Yes, I rang her on Thursday evening.'

'As I was saying,' Colin continued, 'Anthea mentioned it to Paul and he answered sharply, 'I know.' Did you tell him, Emma?'

'I telephoned Paul but he wasn't there. I left a message. He is our conductor, after all. Why does it matter,

Colin?' Emma didn't want to continue this conversation.

'It doesn't. I'm sorry, if I'm asking too many questions.'

'What else happened on Friday?' Emma changed the subject.

'Samantha was in good form. She constantly cracked jokes, which Paul seemed to find very amusing. Since she's been back, he's like a new person.'

'You keep me well informed about Samantha,' Emma remarked. 'Are you sure you don't fancy her yourself?'

'How could you say that? You know I'm only interested in you. Besides, it's Paul that Samantha's after.'

'Colin!'

'All right. I'll say no more. I'd better go now and let you get to bed. Good night, Emma.'

She went to the door with Colin, pulling her dressing gown tightly around her. She stood waving as he walked towards the staircase. Suddenly her heart missed a beat as she saw a tall dark-haired man striding along towards her flat from the other direction. *Paul*, she thought. *What is he doing here?*

Emma stood watching and listening, mesmerised, as the two men nearly collided.

'What are you doing here, Paul?' Colin asked incredulously.

'I could ask you the same question.'

'Er . . . yes, well . . . I've been visiting Emma to make sure she was all right, after the fire at her block of flats.'

'And is she?'

'Yes. Just a bit shocked, I think.'

'Right. Good night Colin,' Paul said dismissively as he marched up to Emma. 'Can I come in?' he asked. 'I won't stay long. I can see you're ready for bed.'

Emma blushed. She wished she'd stayed fully dressed. 'Yes, you'd better. I don't make a habit of entertaining in my dressing gown,' she found herself saying defensively, aware that Colin was standing staring at them, a bemused expression on his face.

'I hope you don't,' Paul said dryly.

She quickly closed the front door and they walked into the lounge and sat facing one another. 'I imagine Colin's wondering what's going on,' Paul continued. 'He didn't look very pleased to see me. Anyway, how are you? No ill effects from the fire?'

'I'm okay, thank you, but I didn't expect to see you here.'

'I bet you didn't. Had a good time with Colin?'

'He was only here for a little while. He came to see if I was all right.'

'So? You can do a lot in a few minutes.'

'We were just talking, if you must know,' Emma snapped, 'but as I've said before, it's none of your business.'

'Now, now, Emma. Don't get cross with me again. I didn't come here for that.'

'What did you come for?' she demanded.

'John rang to discuss the music for our concerts and said that he'd heard there'd been a fire at your block of flats.

He was going to call round to make sure you were all right, but I offered to come instead as I wanted to have a chat with you.'

'How quickly news gets around in Farwell. But John must have wondered why you wanted to have a chat with me.'

'News always spreads fast in country towns,' Paul replied, ignoring Emma's second remark. 'You see how concerned everyone is for your welfare. You don't look overjoyed to see me, though.'

I must be a good actress, Emma decided, *at concealing my real feelings.* She could feel her heart thumping fast, but she answered, 'Should I be?'

'You could at least try to look pleased.'

'Why?' *Here I go again*, she thought, *driving Paul away. What makes me act like this?*

'I didn't have to come here tonight,' he continued.

'So, why did you come? Perhaps you shouldn't have.'

'Look, let's stop this, Emma. Every time we meet, we start to argue.'

'And whose fault is that?'

'Please be quiet and listen. I came here because I wanted to see you and to find out how your grandmother was. Strange as it may seem, I do understand how upset you must have been. My grandmother also had a stroke.'

'Oh. What happened to her?'

'Unfortunately, she died, and my grandfather never got over it. He, too, died of a heart attack a few months later.'

'I'm sorry, Paul.' Emma felt terrible. He'd had such tragedy in his life, and all she'd done was snap at him.

'Now, can we please start again? Tell me all about the fire.'

For the next few minutes they discussed what had happened and then Paul asked, 'Can we have dinner together on Saturday?'

'But Paul, what about your partner?' The words were out before she could stop them.

'My partner! Now what's this non-sense you're talking?' His voice was impatient.

'I rang you on Thursday. I spoke to her on the phone.'

'Oh Emma, that was my mother,' he laughed. 'She'll be very flattered to think that she sounds young enough to be my partner.'

'Well, I didn't know.' Emma could feel her face going crimson.

'I think there's a lot you don't know.'

'What do you mean by that?'

'I'll tell you some time, if we ever do manage to go out together.'

'Samantha won't like it.' She hadn't meant to say that, but she couldn't stop the words from coming.

'Emma, you're not still going on about Samantha! I told you before, she's just a friend. She's on her own and a bit lonely. I know how she feels.'

'You, lonely, Paul? I can't imagine that.'

'You lack imagination, Emma, as I've said before.'

'You've got your mother to talk to, so you shouldn't be lonely.'

'A mother's not the same as a partner. Besides, she's still missing my father.'

Emma didn't know how to reply, so she kept quiet. *I must do this more often*, she thought, *instead of saying the first thing that comes into my head*.

Paul got up and walked around the lounge, looking appreciatively at everything. 'What a lovely flat you have. You didn't give me a chance to say it before. You've so many books.'

'I bought some of them from Kavanagh's.'

'What about this one, Emma?' He selected a book and held it up. 'You didn't get that from my store.'

'Oh, *The Life of our Lord* by Charles Dickens. No, that belonged to my other grandmother. She gave it to me just before she died. She used to read it to me when I was a little girl. I think it was a present from her mother.'

'That's a rare book, you know, Emma.'

'Is it?'

'Yes, Dickens wrote it for his children and used to read it to them, but it was only published once and that was in nineteen thirty-four, sixty-four years after his death.'

'I'll have to look after it then.'

'You should. I've never actually seen a copy before, although I've always wanted to. I enjoy reading Dickens.'

'So do I, especially *A Tale of Two Cities*.'

'There, Emma, we have something in common. That's my favourite Dickens book too.'

'I'd never have thought that you would like Dickens.'

'Why not?'

'Perhaps because a lot of people find Charles Dickens's stories rather slow.'

'Meaning that you think I'm very fast.'

'No, not exactly. Look, I'm very tired. I don't know what I'm saying.'

'I'll take the hint and go. But before I do, will you answer my question? Can we have dinner together next Saturday?'

'Yes, please, Paul.'

'I can't believe it. You said yes! Maybe this time we really will go out together.'

'I hope so.'

'What's happened, Emma? You're not arguing with me.'

'I must be very tired.' She smiled.

'I'll look forward to Friday.' Paul walked to the front door and then stopped. 'I've just remembered — last week at the rehearsal, someone suggested we had a party for Nick Brown, when he comes back to be our soloist in November. What do you think of that?'

'Er . . . it . . . depends when the party is,' Emma prevaricated.

'You don't sound very enthusiastic. Have you met Nick?'

'Yes. I . . . I suppose a party would be a good idea.' Emma tried to appear normal. She didn't want to get into a conversation with Paul about Nick.

'I seem to be the only person who hasn't met him. John's told me what a capable pianist he is, and Samantha's delighted he's coming back. She thinks he's brilliant. What do you think?'

'He is a very good pianist,' Emma answered quickly.

'Good. I'm looking forward to hearing him. I really will go now. Let you get some rest. You sound so tired.' Paul opened the door and called, 'Good night, Emma,' and strode off.

Thank goodness he didn't question me further about Nick. I really wish they'd found someone else to be the soloist. She sighed. *I think there are going to be some embarrassing times ahead.*

7

The next day at school, all the children were very excitable and teaching was difficult. Word had got around about the fire and that Emma lived in the block of flats where it had happened. Everyone wanted to hear the details and she grew tired of reliving the events of the night before.

In the evening when Emma returned from school, she found another letter from Nick. Her first instinct was to destroy it, but in the end, after eating dinner, curiosity got the better of her. She sat down on the sofa and ripped open the envelope. 'What conceit!' she exclaimed as she read it. 'Because I didn't reply to his letter, he thinks I never received it. He just can't get it into his head that I'm no longer interested.'

Nick had ended the letter by saying,

'I can't wait to see you. I'll ring as soon as I arrive in England. Then I can make up for what I did. I'm sure everything will work out fine. Please reply, Emma. Love from Nick.'

'The cheek!' she said aloud in a fit of rage. 'He can wait forever for a reply. He's not going to get one from me.' Emma screwed the letter up and tossed it into the bin.

A few minutes later, the doorbell rang. *Now who can this be? I was hoping for an early night. Maybe it's someone about the fire.* She opened the door and was surprised to see Colin standing there. 'Hello,' she said, trying to appear welcoming. 'Come in. I didn't think I'd see you this evening.'

'I had to make sure you weren't suffering any ill effects from the fire.'

'That's very kind of you Colin, but I'm perfectly all right, thank you.'

'Good.'

'I actually enjoyed being a celebrity at school today,' Emma smiled. 'Everybody wanted to know what had happened.'

'Well, it was quite an event for Farwell. It's not every night that the fire engine's called out. I'm just glad that no one was hurt though. It could have been a real tragedy.'

'I saw the owners of the flat looking at the damage when I came home from school. They were very shocked. They're having to stay with members of their family.'

'It's a good thing it didn't spread to any other flats.'

'I know. I shudder to think what might have happened.'

Colin walked across the room and Emma, suspecting that he was going to put his arm around her, quickly dodged away, suggesting, 'How about a cup of coffee? I was going to make myself one when you came.'

'That would be lovely.' He followed Emma to the kitchen. 'By the way, what did Paul want last night?' he asked. 'I couldn't believe it when I saw him.'

'He was just enquiring about my welfare, like you, Colin.'

'Oh. So he has got a heart after all.'

Emma couldn't help smiling. 'I think so,' she replied.

The two young people spent the next hour in pleasant conversation, discussing the fire, the orchestra, and her day at school. Emma found Colin easy to get on with. She was glad to have his friendship and thought, *If I hadn't met Paul, I might have been more interested in Colin. He's friendly, likeable, solid and dependable — all good qualities — and he genuinely seems to care about me. Paul hasn't checked up on me as Colin has, but he did come round the night before,* she reminded herself. *Colin isn't arrogant, bad-tempered, sarcastic, argumentative and full of his own importance. Is Paul really like that, or is it just my perception of him? Samantha doesn't have any trouble with him. But how do I know that?* Emma asked herself. *Paul told me that he only sees Samantha as a friend. How does she see him? And more importantly, how does Paul see me?* All these questions went round and round in her head, and she could come to no conclusions.

★ ★ ★

On the following Friday evening when Emma walked into the hall for the next rehearsal, she found Paul already there, deep in conversation with Samantha. He seemed completely unaware of Emma's presence.

'Paul's early for once,' Bill joked. 'I wonder what's happened.'

As soon as everyone had arrived, Paul informed them all that John's composition had arrived from the printers. 'I've heard some of the 'Farewell Rhapsody' and think that it will be just perfect for us. It has some really beautiful themes. I think you're going to enjoy playing it. We'll give out the music later so that you can all start practising individually, and we'll commence work on it together the Friday after our concert with Nick Brown.

Next week,' Paul continued, 'we'll be starting to learn the Christmas music from Handel's 'Messiah', which we'll be performing with the choir from Farwell Parish Church at their carol service. So as you can see, we have a very busy schedule ahead of us.'

The rehearsal passed quickly. Paul seemed relaxed and there was a good atmosphere amongst all the members of the orchestra. The only thing worrying Emma was that Paul had completely ignored her throughout the whole evening. She began to think that he regretted inviting her out to dinner.

However, at the end, when everyone was packing up, he called to her, 'Emma, can I have a word with you, please?'

'What have you done?' Bill teased.

'Be quiet,' Anthea urged. 'Don't worry the poor girl. Paul probably wants to have a chat about the music, as she's missed some of the rehearsals.' She turned to Emma. 'Take no notice of Bill. He likes to have a joke.'

It was very noisy in the hall, and no one heard Paul arranging to call for Emma at seven thirty the following evening.

'Is everything all right?' Colin asked as she returned to her place.

'Yes, of course,' she answered quickly, her cheeks glowing as Colin gave her a surprised look and Anthea eyed her speculatively.

The sun was shining when Emma awoke on Saturday morning. She got out of bed with the eager anticipation that this was going to be a special day for her. She telephoned her parents and was reassured that all was well with them, and that her grandmother was continuing to make good progress.

'Are you doing anything exciting today, dear?' Her mother asked.

'No,' she lied. Emma wasn't going to mention Paul yet. She was too uncertain about what the future held for them. *After all, we might only go on this one date*, she thought, but her heart sank at that prospect. *I mustn't drive him away. I will have to try and stay calm. It's so strange how I react to Paul. I don't usually lose my temper as quickly. Most of my friends would probably say I was quite easy-going, but I'm definitely not with him.*

The day seemed to drag, but at last it was time to get ready. Emma had decided that she would wear a new pink shift dress and matching jacket, which she felt fitted her perfectly. She had a leisurely bath, liberally sprayed herself with an exotic perfume, and tried to put on her make-up with a steady hand, but found it was trembling. *I'm acting like a schoolgirl again. Anyone would think I'd never been on a date before. Paul is the only man, though, who has had this effect on me. I didn't get in this state over Nick, even when I thought I was in love with him.*

The doorbell rang at exactly seven thirty. Emma, who had been ready for the past half hour, opened the door nervously, her heart pounding. She stifled a gasp of delight as she saw Paul standing there in his immaculate navy suit and gleaming white shirt. He smiled and said, 'Emma, you look lovely. What a beautiful shade of pink.'

'Thank you, Paul,' she replied, feeling too shy to tell him that he also looked terrific.

'I thought we would drive to a rather nice restaurant I know a few miles outside of Farwell, if that's all right with you.'

'Yes, that sounds fine,' Emma answered, following him to his black Mercedes, remembering the first time she had seen him and his car. It all seemed so long ago now, that day when she had bumped into him in the car park after her audition with John Grant, but it was barely two months.

Emma climbed into Paul's car, revelling in the luxury. 'This is a lot more comfortable than my old Mini,' she remarked foolishly. *What a silly thing to say*, she thought. *Of course it is.*

'I should hope so,' Paul replied.

Emma sat beside him, wondering what to talk about, but after a few minutes she relaxed, noting that Paul's face was not at all forbidding, as it sometimes was at their rehearsals. She told herself to enjoy the evening and soon they were exchanging pleasantries.

Paul parked the car outside an already crowded seventeenth-century inn. 'I've booked a table for eight o' clock,' he said. 'It gets very busy in here.'

Emma could understand why as she walked through the doorway. In spite of its age, no expense had been spared on the luxurious furnishings, lush carpet, and the reproduction old masters' paintings on the walls. 'What a wonderful place,' she breathed.

'I'm glad you approve. I think you'll like the food, too,' Paul assured her as the restaurant manager came over to greet them.

'Good evening, Mr. Kavanagh, how nice to see you again. That's a pleasure we have infrequently these days.'

'I'll have to try and remedy that situation,' Paul smiled.

'I'm very pleased to meet you, madam,' the manager said, turning to Emma and shaking her hand. 'I've reserved you a cosy window table.'

Emma couldn't help wondering who else Paul had brought there in the past. She knew it wasn't Samantha, though, as the manager had stated that Paul hadn't been there for some time.

When they were seated, Emma glanced around at her fellow diners who were all very well dressed. She felt relieved that she too had made a special effort. She perused the menu, but couldn't decide what to have. 'It all sounds so delicious,' she murmured.

'Let me choose for you, then,' Paul suggested.

Emma eagerly agreed to this.

A young waitress came over to their table and smiled broadly at Paul. 'Mr. Kavanagh, lovely to see you again. It's so long since you've been in here. We wondered what had happened to you.

Are you still lecturing at the university?'

'Not any more, but I keep busy,' he answered shortly.

That waitress fancies Paul, Emma thought. *She keeps giving me envious glances. She seems to know a lot about him.* 'So you used to be a university lecturer? What was your subject?' Emma enquired.

'Music.'

'Why did you give it up?'

'I had no choice. I had to when I took over Kavanagh's.'

'Oh, of course.' Emma felt annoyed with herself for asking that question.

The wine waiter brought their drinks and Paul said, 'Now Emma, tell me about yourself. All I know is that you're a teacher and you have a grandmother who's had a stroke.'

'There's not much to tell,' she answered.

'I'm sure there's plenty. For a start, how have you managed to remain single for so long?'

'Thanks,' Emma interrupted. 'You

make me sound like an old woman. I'm only twenty-five!'

'You didn't let me finish. I was about to say that with your looks, I'm surprised someone hasn't snapped you up already.'

Emma blushed and replied without thinking, 'I could say the same about you.'

Paul seemed not to hear and continued, 'I'm sure Colin isn't the only one whose heart you've broken, if what you're telling me is true, and you really have no interest in him.'

'I was speaking the truth,' Emma protested. 'I don't know why you find it so hard to believe, but can we please not spend the evening talking about Colin? I haven't broken his or anyone else's heart.'

'I'm not so sure about that.'

'Well, I am,' Emma retorted. 'Now, can I ask you a question?'

'Okay.'

'When I met you in Kavanagh's Bookstore that day, you told me you hadn't expected to inherit it and that life didn't always turn out the way we wanted. What did you mean?'

'Just that. I'm sorry Emma, but I don't want to talk about it.' His face had become serious and brooding. 'Let's enjoy the moment and forget about the darker side of life.'

Emma wondered what it was that had hurt him so badly. She was torn between feeling sympathy and also anger that he didn't trust her enough to tell her what was troubling him. What was he talking about when he referred to the darker side of life? Had he confided in Samantha? Then Emma thought, *I've been hurt by Nick, and I haven't wanted to talk to Paul about it, so why should he want to tell me? We still hardly know one another.*

'What made you come and live in Farwell?' Paul was asking, his face no longer shadowed.

'When I'd nearly finished my teacher training, they were advertising for newly qualified teachers in Farwell. I visited the town, liked it and applied for the job, and was lucky enough to get it. I love it here. Although it's not a large town, it has everything you need, including the university.'

'And Kavanagh's Bookstore,' Paul smiled.

'Yes, of course, I mustn't forget that,' Emma agreed.

'And the symphony orchestra. Not all towns are as lucky,' he added.

'Do you live in Farwell, Paul?'

'No, in Lynsford. It's about five miles away.'

'Oh, I haven't been there. You live with your mother?'

'Yes, as you know.'

'Did you decide to live with her when your father died?'

'Something like that,' he murmured.

Emma was having difficulty in getting Paul to talk about himself. What was the mystery surrounding him? Hadn't Bill called him the mystery man, too? Would she ever be able to break through his reserve?

The waitress brought their first course. She kept smiling at Paul but largely ignored Emma, who was desperately trying to think of something interesting to say. The evening was not going as well as she hoped. Paul looked thoughtful, even sad, and she wished that she could help him in some way.

The meal was excellent. They both ate slowly, savouring each mouthful, making polite small talk. The waitress kept hovering around, asking Paul if everything was all right, and whether she could get them anything else. Emma would have preferred it if she'd left them in peace.

'She fancies you,' Emma burst out, and then regretted it.

Paul just smiled and answered, 'Don't worry about her. She's like that with all the men.'

'Who said I was worrying?' Emma exclaimed. She wanted to ask Paul how he came to be the conductor of Farwell Symphony Orchestra, but sensed this was not the time for further questioning. *Perhaps another time*, she thought, *if there is one.*

'That was wonderful,' Emma sighed as she put down her spoon. 'The peach meringue was out of this world and the lamb was so tender. I've never eaten such a delicious meal.'

'I thought you'd like it. Shall we have coffee?'

As they were drinking, Emma wished she could be more like Samantha, continually making witty remarks. Paul was always laughing when he was with her, but this evening he seemed to be in a sombre mood, as if there was something on his mind. Emma wondered what it could be, but was too nervous to ask. She didn't want to do or say anything else that could upset Paul.

'It's a lovely evening. How about a stroll beside the river?' he suggested. Emma agreed.

She glanced up at Paul's face from time to time as they were walking, but it was inscrutable. They talked about music and the orchestra, but nothing very personal.

'I'll be visiting my parents at half term,' Emma told Paul. 'What will you be doing?'

'Nothing much, apart from working at the store.'

Of, course. He doesn't get half term holidays like me. Why do I keep making these inane remarks? Emma asked herself.

'You're not going to any more barn dances, I hope?' Paul said sarcastically. 'You'll have to be careful if you do.'

She blushed furiously and was about to tell him to mind his own business, when she thought better of it and answered, 'I'm not planning on going to any more at the moment.'

Paul looked at his watch. 'It's getting late. Time I took Cinderella home, if she's to get there before midnight.'

'Yes, you won't want me turning into a pumpkin, or something worse,' she smiled.

They returned to his car and drove quickly back to Farwell. Paul escorted Emma up to her flat. At the front door, he clasped her hand briefly, saying, 'I have enjoyed this evening. We must do it again some time. Take care, Emma.'

She replied, 'Thank you for a lovely time.'

'Good night,' he called as he hurried along the landing.

Emma went inside and sank down onto her sofa. 'What an evening!' she murmured aloud. *I feel as if I have been pulled through a hedge backwards. That wasn't the most successful date I have been on. Paul revealed little of himself, and I've no idea what he was really thinking. Was he just being polite when he said he'd enjoyed the evening? He didn't suggest a date for us to go out together again.* Emma also had mixed feelings about the fact that he'd behaved like a perfect gentleman, and hadn't even tried to kiss her. She wasn't sure if she would have been pleased or disappointed if he had. Then the thought crossed her mind that if Paul had been with Samantha, she would probably have kissed him.

★   ★   ★

Emma spent the next few days hoping that Paul would ring, but he didn't. *I don't seem to learn,* she thought. *After all the sleepless nights I had getting over Nick, I didn't intend to go through that again, but I can't seem to help myself. Now I'm constantly thinking about Paul.*

By the time Friday evening arrived, Emma was convinced that she had ruined everything on her date with Paul by asking him too many questions, and that he had lost interest in her. This idea was confirmed at the rehearsal, where she observed that Samantha was constantly at his side.

Even Bill noticed. 'Look at Sam,' he commented. 'I've never seen her like this before. She's really besotted with

Paul. She won't leave him alone for a minute.'

'He doesn't seem to mind,' Colin replied.

Emma kept quiet, thinking, *I had my chance, but I blew it. I can't compete with Samantha. She's too much for me. All the men have been ogling her tonight, in her short lemon skirt, and Paul's as bad. She's lapping it all up.*

To Emma's relief, Colin didn't press his attentions on her, and when it was time to leave she tried to creep away unnoticed.

Paul spotted her, however, and called out, 'Don't go without saying goodbye. You're not avoiding me, are you? You haven't spoken to me all evening.'

'I didn't get a chance,' she replied bitterly. 'You were otherwise engaged.'

Paul gave Emma a look of surprise. 'I suppose you're referring to Samantha. She's finding life rather tough at the moment, and needed someone to jolly her along.'

'She didn't look very miserable to

me, laughing and joking all the time,' Emma muttered.

'That's how she copes. I was just trying to help. Listen, I want to ask you something . . . '

Before he could continue, Samantha had come across and grabbed his arm, completely ignoring Emma. She could hear him groaning under his breath as Sam said, 'Paul, there's something I must tell you.'

Sam dragged him away as Emma turned from him in disgust, mumbling, 'Good night, Paul.'

He replied, 'Just a minute, Sam,' and then called, 'Emma, don't go.'

She stopped and was about to walk back to him, when she heard Sam saying, 'Let her go, Paul. I need to talk to you now.'

Emma pretended not to hear and hurried outside. As she got into her car, she thought, *Why did I do that? It'll be another two weeks before I see Paul, as it's half term next week. He wanted to ask me something. Perhaps he was going to invite me to go out with him again and I ran off like a frightened rabbit. If I want Paul, I can see that I'm going to have to fight for him. But what chance do I have against Samantha? I act like a silly schoolgirl most of the time. Sam hardly knows I exist. She certainly doesn't see me as a threat.*

* * *

During the half-term holiday from school, Emma went to stay with her parents. Her brother Ben was there, too. He couldn't stop talking about his latest girlfriend. 'Haven't you met anyone special yet?' Ben asked.

'No,' Emma answered, quickly changing the conversation. 'How's Gran?'

'Doing very well,' her father replied.

Emma enjoyed this time with her family, although her mind was often elsewhere, dwelling on the meal she had with Paul and her last meeting with him at the rehearsal, where Samantha was monopolising him. She wondered if

Sam had got her way with Paul at last. Maybe he would be taking her out. Emma was sure she could be very persuasive and Paul might find it hard to resist. After all, she was extremely attractive.

★ ★ ★

A few days later Emma returned to her flat. She immediately switched on her answer phone to see if there were any messages and was very disappointed to find there were none. Most of her friends knew her mobile number and she'd received text messages from them whilst she'd been away, but she'd never given Paul that number. She'd been hoping that he would have tried to contact her, but he hadn't. She feared he might be too busy with Samantha.

Emma went back to work and soon got immersed in school life. Whenever she had a spare moment in the evenings, she kept up her violin practice. She wanted to make sure that she could play all the music competently.

On Friday evening, she arrived early for the rehearsal. From her car, she could see Bill and Anthea deep in conversation as they walked towards the hall. *They seem to be getting on well these days*, she thought.

She stepped out of her car, and Colin came over. 'Hello, Emma. It seems ages since I've seen you. Did you have a good half term?'

'Yes, thank you. Did you?'

'I still had to go to work. Not all of us get long holidays, you know.'

'Sorry, I forgot.'

'One evening last week, when I was out having a drink with a mate, guess who I saw.'

'I don't know,' Emma answered, hoping he wasn't going to tell her that he'd seen Paul with Samantha.

'It was Rob.'

'Oh.'

'It's all right, Emma. I think you've got rid of him. He was with a blonde. They were both so wrapped up in each other that he didn't notice me.'

'Good. I mean, I'm glad he's found someone.'

'I thought you would be.'

As they entered the hall, there was a hubbub of noise as members of the orchestra were chatting to each other and tuning their instruments. Bill waved and beckoned to them. He was standing talking to Anthea. 'Colin, Emma, come over here,' he called.

Emma whispered, 'I wonder what they're up to. They look very excited about something.'

'Hello, Bill. It's good to see you and you too, Anthea,' Colin greeted them. 'What's up?'

'Haven't you heard what's happened?' Anthea asked.

'No, I don't think so. Tell us.'

'Well as we were on our way in, we met John and he told us that he was in charge tonight.'

'Why's that?' Colin interrupted.

'Paul can't come. John says he's at the hospital.'

8

Whatever can have happened? Emma thought. *Paul's at the hospital. Is he ill, or had an accident, or is it his mother?*

'Oh, I hope it's nothing serious,' Colin exclaimed.

'We don't know. That's all John told us. He rushed off to get ready for the rehearsal. Perhaps he will tell us more when we get started.'

Emma felt desperately worried so she kept quiet, not wanting to betray her feelings to anyone.

A few minutes later, John called everyone to order. 'As most of you will have heard by now, Paul will not be here tonight, so I am taking the rehearsal.'

'What's happened?' a latecomer called.

'Paul's at the hospital.'

At that moment Samantha entered the hall, teetering on high heels, her long, blonde hair streaming behind in a golden halo. 'What did you say?' she asked.

'Paul's at the hospital,' John repeated.

'Oh no,' she gasped, her face going pale. 'Is he ill? What's happened?'

'No, I don't think he's ill,' John replied, 'but I'm not sure what's up. Paul left a message on my answer phone, saying that he wouldn't be able to come tonight. He asked me to take over for him. He's going to try and ring me at the weekend to let me know what's going on.'

'How did Paul sound?' Samantha still appeared shocked.

'It's hard to say. The answer phone distorts people's voices, but I think he was very worried.'

'Oh dear. I'll have to ring Paul. I do hope it's nothing dreadful.' Samantha took her violin out of its case and started to tune it. 'I suppose we'd better carry on with our practice. It's the least we can do.'

'You're right, Sam,' John answered.

'It's no good us speculating about Paul. None of us knows what's happened, so we should do as he said and get on with the rehearsal.'

There was a buzz of noise around the hall as everyone digested this information and began to tune their instruments.

Emma had listened to all this while feeling sick inside, hoping desperately that it wasn't Paul who was ill or had been in an accident. Her only consolation was that Samantha also didn't know any more details than the rest of them, so maybe she hadn't seen Paul during the half-term break either. Emma had to keep a tight rein on her feelings so that no one would suspect her involvement with Paul. Everyone knew that Samantha was interested in him, so they were not surprised that she was upset.

Emma guessed that it was Paul's mother who was ill, but wondered why he hadn't told John that. It would have put an end to all their discussions about him, but Paul never did the expected thing. He seemed to make a habit of being unpredictable.

Samantha's going to phone Paul. So why shouldn't I do the same? Emma reasoned. *Will he be pleased if I do, or will he just think that I am checking up on him to be nosy?* Those thoughts went round and round in her head. *Paul didn't want to talk about himself when we had dinner together, so he might resent being questioned now. It's as Bill said. Paul seems to enjoy being a mystery man. But I can't just ignore him when he has a problem. He was kind to me after the fire. I've got to see if I can help.*

Suddenly it occurred to Emma that Samantha was worried Paul might be ill. She never made any mention of his mother. Did that mean she didn't know Paul lived with her?

'Wake up, Emma. You haven't tuned your violin yet.' Anthea broke into her reverie. 'You look miles away. I can see John's nearly ready to start.'

'Oh, sorry. I . . . I'm just a bit tired. I'll do it now.' Emma picked up her violin and tried to rid her mind of all these thoughts. *I've got to concentrate on the present*, she told herself.

'Have you had a difficult week at school?' Anthea asked.

'It's always hard going back after a holiday. It takes a while for the children to get back into their normal routine.'

'Yes, I can imagine that.'

'This is a particularly busy half term,' Emma continued, 'as we're starting to get ready for Christmas. Oh, I've just remembered, I was going to ask Bill and John and maybe one or two other people if they could come and play their instruments to the children at my school.'

'Did I hear my name mentioned?' Bill asked.

After Emma had explained everything to him, he replied, 'That's a great idea. I'd be delighted to come. I'm sure the others will be too. Leave it all to me, I'll sort it out for you.'

Emma thanked him. *They're a nice crowd*, she thought gratefully. Then, catching sight of Colin staring across at her, she gave him a smile, hoping that he hadn't noticed her worried face.

An elderly flautist stood up and said, 'John, before we start, may I congratulate you on your composition. I've tried my part and it's really good. I love the main theme. I can't wait to hear the whole thing.'

'Neither can I,' Bill joined in. 'You've done us proud, John.'

'Here, here,' other members chorused, and a spontaneous burst of applause echoed round the hall.

'Thank you very much, everyone. It's so kind of you, but you should reserve your judgement until you have heard the whole work.' John looked embarrassed. 'I suggest before we start, we make a date for the party we're giving for Nick Brown.'

That was the last thing Emma wanted to think about. If only there was some way of getting out of it. Maybe she could excuse herself and say that she had to visit her gran on that date? Lots of people in the orchestra knew about her grandmother's stroke, so they would think it was a genuine reason for not attending.

There was much deliberation and discussion. Finally it was decided that the best time for the party would be immediately after the next concert, when everybody would be feeling in a celebratory mood. Emma, however, was not pleased about this. Now she knew there was no way she could get out of it, and she would have to face Nick in front of Paul and the rest of the orchestra. She wondered if Paul liked parties. She couldn't imagine him relaxing enough to let his hair down. Then the thought struck her that if it was Paul who was ill, he might not be at the party. Emma quickly dismissed this idea, telling herself that it must be his mother who was in hospital. She hoped the poor woman would make a speedy recovery.

The rest of the rehearsal passed uneventfully. John was a good conductor who brought out the best in the orchestra, but he didn't have the fire and passion which Paul displayed on occasions. When they had finished, Colin asked Emma to have coffee with him, but she refused, saying she was very tired.

He scrutinised her face intently and said, 'You've never really recovered from the flu. I think you're working too hard.'

'I've no choice,' she replied. 'School takes up all my energy, but perhaps we can go another time,' she suggested when she saw Colin's disappointed face.

'I'd like that,' he answered.

* * *

The next day, Emma tried to telephone Paul, but on hearing his answer phone she lost courage and hung up. The same thing happened again the following day.

Then she gave up. Emma justified her actions by telling herself that if Paul wanted to, he could have rung her. The fact that no one had answered the telephone confirmed her suspicion that it was Paul's mother who was ill in hospital. Emma wondered if Samantha had been more successful with her phone calls. She guessed that Sam would have left a message rather than hanging up like a frightened child.

On Wednesday Emma had to call in to Kavanagh's Bookstore to buy some stationery for school. She walked in nervously, half expecting to see Paul, but there was no sign of him. She made her purchases and was on her way out, when she spotted Samantha browsing amongst the paperbacks. She was wearing an elegant tangerine suit, looking breathtakingly beautiful. Emma thought, *How could Paul not be in love with someone so attractive? What chance do I have of competing with Samantha?*

Emma tried to creep away unnoticed,

but Sam called, 'Emma, what a surprise seeing you in here.' She reluctantly walked over. After a brief conversation, Samantha confided, 'I'm very worried about Paul. I've tried ringing, but there was no reply, so I left a message. He hasn't rung back though. I can't think what's happened. I was hoping to see him in here. I was told by his manager that he hasn't been in all week and they are not sure when he's going to return.'

Emma didn't tell her that she, too, had rung Paul and also had received no reply. She wondered what Sam's reaction would have been if she had known. She replied, 'I expect we'll hear something on Friday. I'm sure John will tell us.' Emma tried to sound nonchalant. *This is the longest conversation I've ever had with Sam*, she thought. *I'm sure she doesn't know about my date with Paul. She wouldn't be talking to me like this if she did.*

Although Emma was equally worried about Paul, she believed she'd managed to conceal it from Sam, and was relieved that Samantha knew no more than she did. So, maybe Paul was telling the truth when he said there was nothing going on between him and Sam. Perhaps it was just wishful thinking on her part. Then Emma thought if Paul was at the hospital during the daytime as well as in the evening, his mother must be in a very bad way.

* * *

On Friday at the next rehearsal, all the members of the orchestra including Samantha arrived punctually. It was only the two conductors who were missing. Nobody had heard any more news and Samantha was still bemoaning that fact. 'Whatever has happened to Paul?' she kept saying. 'I do hope he's all right. I tried phoning him but got no reply.'

'John's sure to know,' Bill reassured her. 'I'm sure he'll be here soon. Maybe Paul will be back too.'

'I do hope so,' Samantha replied.

Then Bill whispered to Anthea and Emma, 'I'm really surprised Paul hasn't been in touch with Sam. I thought they were going out together.'

A few minutes later John walked in with a grim face.

'What is it?' Bill asked. 'You look as if you've seen a ghost.'

'Well, I've had a bit of a shock. I've been speaking to Paul on the telephone.'

'Go on, tell us about it,' Samantha urged, also turning pale. 'Is he coming tonight?'

'No, he — '

'Is he ill?' Samantha interrupted. 'Oh please don't say he is.'

'No, Paul's not ill, but he can't come tonight because he's . . . in London at a hospital with his . . . his daughter.'

9

'His what? I must have misheard. I thought you said his daughter,' Samantha shrieked.

'No, you were right, that's what I said. Paul's at a London hospital with his daughter,' John confirmed. 'She was taken there from his local hospital by ambulance.'

There was a sudden hum of startled conversation buzzing round the hall.

'But that can't be true,' Samantha wailed. 'He's never told me about her.'

'I don't think any of us knew,' John answered. 'I was as surprised as you when he told me, but I suppose I ought not to have been. There's no reason why he shouldn't have a family. It's just that he hasn't mentioned one before.'

'You think he's married? You think he's got a wife?' Samantha shouted.

'Oh . . . the . . . the cheat, the liar. He's been leading me on, letting me think he was free and single, when all the time he's been living with his wife.'

'I didn't say that. I don't know whether he has a wife,' John tried to console her.

'I just can't believe it,' Samantha exclaimed, throwing her music down in a fit of temper. 'Men! Why do I bother? I should have realised that with my luck, someone so good-looking would have to be married. How could he do this to me, though? Not telling me he had a daughter.' She stomped around, beside herself with rage, repeating, 'How *could* he?'

'Don't get hysterical, Sam. There's probably some good explanation.' Bill tried to calm her and Anthea put an arm around her shoulders.

'It's all right for you to say that. You're not the one who's been deceived,' Sam retorted.

'Stop upsetting yourself,' Anthea urged. 'We don't know the facts yet. As

Bill said, I'm sure Paul hasn't been deliberately devious. He must have his reasons for saying nothing.' She turned to John. 'What's wrong with Paul's daughter? Do you know? It must be bad if she's been taken to a London hospital. Don't judge Paul too harshly, Sam. We don't know the full story. Anyway, we shouldn't be bothering about his private life at the moment. We ought to be more concerned about his child.'

'Well spoken, Anthea,' Bill joined in. 'I agree with you. Do you know any more, John?'

'No, not really. Only that she's having tests and it sounds pretty serious.'

'Oh dear. I hope she'll be all right. Poor Paul, he must be out of his mind with worry,' Anthea murmured.

'He is,' John answered. 'Paul's a very private man, never giving anything away about his personal life. Although I've been out with him for a drink on several occasions, he doesn't seem to like talking about himself, so I haven't pressed him. Tonight when he rang, I think he felt obliged to tell me about his child. He just said that his daughter lived with him and his mother.'

'And his wife?' Samantha asked.

'As I told you before, I don't know if he has one,' John replied. 'I'm sorry I can't tell you any more.' He tapped his baton firmly on the stand and immediately a hushed silence fell round the hall. 'Look everyone, I realise this has come as a shock to you, but Paul's private life and what he does in his own time is no concern of ours. He's a good conductor and I'm sure he's a decent man. Let's show a bit of compassion towards him.'

'Here, here,' Bill agreed. 'You're right, John. What can we do to help?'

'Well, I think we should carry on with our rehearsal. I'll try to keep in touch with Paul this week and we'll all have to hope for the best. He said he would ring me in a few days to let me know what was happening. So I suggest we stop gossiping and turn to the first page

170

of the 'Egmont Overture' and start practising.'

'Quite right. You keep us in order.' A cellist backed John up. 'We've got to give Paul a chance. We're here to make music, not pick someone to pieces.'

Samantha sat down, seeming subdued after hearing those words, as if she regretted her outburst.

'Now, if you could all finish tuning your instruments, we'll get started.' Within a few minutes, John raised his baton and the rehearsal began.

Emma had been watching and listening to everything quietly as if in a dream. *Paul has a daughter* was echoing round and round in her head. She repeated Samantha's question. *Why didn't he tell me? Who is the child's mother? Is she Paul's wife or . . . or . . . his . . . mistress? But he said he has no wife. Is he divorced? Was he widowed? Oh, if that's the case, the poor child has no mother. How terrible! I wonder how old the girl is. Now, at least, I understand why Paul lives with his mother — so she can help him look after his daughter. But why didn't he tell me about her? Could it be that he isn't divorced? He's still living with his wife, or he never married the child's mother? So many questions, and no answers.*

Emma was upset to think that yet again Paul hadn't trusted her enough to confide in her. The only consolation was that he hadn't told Samantha either. She tried to concentrate on playing the violin, but found the music tedious, and she longed for the rehearsal to be over. Usually she enjoyed every minute, but there was too much going on inside her head. *Pull yourself together*, she urged. *Stop thinking about your problems. There's a young child seriously ill in hospital, who may not recover. Imagine how Paul must be feeling now. What can I do for him? I could telephone, Emma decided. Offer to help in any way he wants. Maybe cook Paul a meal? Or just be there for him if he needs someone to talk to. Would he want that? He was kind to me when he heard about my grandmother being ill, and he made sure I was all right after the fire at the block of flats. I can't just ignore him now. I'll ring.* But there had been no reply when she'd tried last week, Emma remembered. *So, I'll try again,* she resolved. *I wish I'd persevered last time. If I'd left a message maybe he would have got back to me.*

The rehearsal dragged on and on. John did his best, but no one's heart was really in it. John chivvied them along. 'We've only got two more weeks till our concert with Nick Brown. We need to do better than this. We don't want to let Paul down.'

Nick! Emma thought. *He'll be here soon. I've enough to worry about without thinking of him. I hope he doesn't get in touch with me, but I bet he will.*

During the interval, Colin came over to Emma and said, 'That was a surprise about Paul having a daughter. I always thought he was a bit of a dark horse. I wonder what else he's hiding from us. Do you think he has a wife?'

'I really don't know, Colin, but instead of speculating about his personal life, we should be more concerned about his child and what's wrong with her,' Emma snapped.

'Yes, you're right. I was being thoughtless. I shouldn't have said that.'

'No, you shouldn't.'

'Oh Emma, you're giving me such disapproving looks. I feel like a naughty child in front of his teacher,' Colin smiled.

Before she could make further comment, Emma was relieved to see Anthea, who had come across wanting to join in their conversation.

'You know, Paul's so different from his father,' she said. 'Hubert was open and friendly, easy to get on with. There was nothing mysterious about him. It's terrible the way he died so suddenly. He wasn't old.'

'I didn't know Paul's father. What

happened?' Colin enquired.

Anthea told him all she knew and then continued, 'Maybe that's why Paul is rather cool and aloof. He's still suffering with shock from the death of his father. It is strange, though, that we haven't seen Chris his brother recently. You would have thought that with his father dying, he would have put in an appearance in Kavanagh's. I wonder what's happened to him. Perhaps he's moved, or emigrated.'

'Well, if you want to know, you'll have to ask Paul,' Bill interrupted. 'But I doubt you'll get an answer, particularly now he's got other things on his mind.'

'Bill, I'm not that tactless. I wouldn't dream of asking Paul anything while he's so worried,' Anthea chided.

Emma was watching Samantha, who although she had calmed down, was looking very dejected and constantly stirring her tea.

'You'll wear that spoon away, Sam,' Bill told her.

'Oh yes, sorry, I wasn't thinking.' All her usual boisterousness had gone and she was very quiet for the remainder of the evening.

Before they went home, Bill told Emma that he'd made arrangements with John and two other elderly members of the orchestra to give a musical recital to the children at her school. 'We can talk about our instruments and show the children how we play them, and we can perform some simple songs for them to sing,' Bill added.

'That will be lovely. Thank you so much.' Emma tried to sound enthusiastic, thrusting thoughts about Paul, his daughter and Samantha from her mind. 'I'll tell the Head when I go to school on Monday,' she informed them.

As Emma was packing her violin into its case, Anthea whispered, 'I've never seen Sam so upset before, not even when she was going through her divorce.'

'What did you say?' Bill leaned across

to try and hear.

'I've never seen Sam in such a state before,' she repeated.

'No,' Bill replied. 'I haven't either. She bounced back quickly after her divorce. I wonder if she will this time. She's always so full of self-confidence. Sam's taken it really badly about Paul having a daughter. He'll have a lot of explaining to do, to satisfy her.'

'Yes, he will,' Anthea answered.

Emma was thinking, *I suppose she feels let down by him. So do I. Samantha doesn't have much luck with men either, like me. We've got that much in common. She's had a divorce and I've had a broken love affair.* Emma almost felt sorry for Sam. *I understand what she's going through and so do the others, but I have to conceal my feelings from everyone. No one must know how I feel about Paul.*

That night, Emma debated with herself what to do. Her earlier resolve to contact Paul was weakening and she was feeling uncertain about doing it. *Dare I phone him? Will he be pleased if I do, or will he think I'm interfering? I wonder what Samantha will do.* Finally, Emma fell asleep after she'd taken a strong line with herself and made a firm resolution to ring Paul once more. *If there's no reply, I will leave a message this time*, she vowed.

The next day Emma couldn't stop her mind from dwelling on the events of the past few weeks. She had decided to telephone Paul on Sunday evening. Things might be more settled with his daughter by then, she reasoned. He should have returned from London, ready for work on Monday, unless of course there was no improvement in his daughter's condition. Emma pushed that idea from her head. It was too awful to contemplate.

She had ambivalent feelings towards Paul, however. She was still annoyed that he hadn't told her about his child and her mother. At the same time, she knew how worried he must be, and so she felt a great deal of sympathy for him.

As Emma nervously dialled Paul's number, her heart was beating fast. *Will he answer, or will it be his mother? What might Paul say? Will he think I'm intruding? After all, John told us that Paul was reluctant to let the orchestra know why he was missing rehearsals. John had persuaded him that it was probably better to inform everyone, otherwise they would think he was just making up excuses not to attend.*

Emma waited, hoping to hear Paul's voice, but instead after a short time his answering machine came on and she was urged to leave a message.

She spoke briefly, saying that she was sorry his daughter was ill and asked if there was anything she could do to help him.

On Monday evening, Emma was sitting on the sofa balancing a pile of books on her lap as she marked them. The telephone rang. She picked up the receiver absent-mindedly, whilst continuing to peruse the books. She was concentrating on deciphering the almost illegible, childish handwriting in front of her. Her heart missed a beat when she heard Paul's voice.

'Emma, thank you for ringing me.'

'Oh Paul,' she hesitated, 'How's your . . . er . . . daughter?'

'We hope she's over the worst now.'

Who's 'we'? Emma thought, but replied, 'Good. What was wrong with her?'

'We're not sure. It was probably a virus. She's had lots of tests and the doctors say there'll be no lasting damage.'

'I'm so pleased, Paul. You must be feeling very relieved.'

'I am.'

'When did you get back?'

'I drove straight to Kavanagh's from London this morning and have just got home and found your message. I rang John to see how the rehearsal went on Friday. He told me everything was fine.'

'Yes, it was,' Emma confirmed. She didn't tell Paul about the strained atmosphere or about Samantha's outburst. 'John worked us all very hard. Which hospital was your daughter in, Paul?'

'Great Ormond Street. She was transferred from our local hospital as they weren't sure what was wrong and the doctor thought they'd have a better idea there. They were brilliant. Couldn't do enough for her. If . . . if she hadn't been taken there, I . . . I . . . ' Paul's voice faltered. 'I don't know what would have happened.'

'It must have been terrible for you,' Emma sympathised, feeling close to tears herself. 'I'm so glad she's getting better.'

'It's such a relief,' Paul sighed. 'I was so worried.'

'I can imagine.'

'Look, Emma, it's nice to talk to you, but I'll have to go. I need some sleep.' She could hear him yawning. 'I've hardly had any the past ten days.'

'Yes, of course. Thank you for calling me back. Keep in touch and let me know if I can do anything.'

'Thank you, Emma. By the way, my daughter's name is Fleur. I'll ring again in a day or two.'

'What a pretty name. I'll look forward to hearing from you. Good night, Paul.'

Emma hung up, feeling elated. Paul had rung her! She wondered if he'd also telephoned Samantha. If he had, she didn't think Sam would have given him a very good reception. *I don't know if Sam will ever forgive Paul for not telling her about Fleur. Have I forgiven him?* Emma asked herself. *I suppose I have. I can't get him out of my system. I would like to know, though, what has happened to the child's mother. I'll just have to be patient and maybe Paul will tell me one day.*

The next evening Paul rang again. 'We need to talk,' he told Emma. 'Can I come round and see you after work tomorrow?' he asked.

'Yes, of course. I'll cook something for you.'

'Thank you. That will be nice. I'll see you at eight.'

Before she could say anything else Paul had hung up.

★   ★   ★

Emma hurried home from school. On the way she purchased a frozen pizza, a quiche, a tub of coleslaw, a fancy loaf of bread and some salad leaves. These would have to suffice for Paul's supper. There was no time to prepare anything more elaborate. She already had some cartons of fruit juice and a bottle of wine in the fridge.

Emma tidied her flat, laid the table and had a long, luxurious bath. She changed into a pale blue skirt and matching top. She was looking forward to seeing Paul, but at the same time she was very nervous and anxious that everything would go well this time. *I must try to keep my tongue in check tonight and refrain from arguing*, she told herself.

At exactly eight o' clock, Paul arrived. He was always on time when seeing her, Emma reflected; yet at the orchestra rehearsals he'd often been late. She ushered him in, noting his tired, drawn face, which somehow seemed to make him even more attractive.

Paul was carrying some pink roses, which he thrust into her hands, saying, 'These are to thank you for providing me with supper. I've come straight from Kavanagh's. I had to catch up on all the paperwork. There was so much to do, as I wasn't there last week. It's amazing how it all builds up.'

'I suppose it must. Thank you for the flowers. They're lovely. Sit down and I'll get you a drink.'

'A fruit juice would be fine. I don't want anything alcoholic. I've got to drive home soon. I can't stay late as I need to see my mother before she goes to bed. She's been in London at the hospital today. They're thinking of letting Fleur come home on Friday.'

'Oh, that's good.'

'I'll have to drive to London to fetch her, but I should be back in time for the rehearsal. Our soloist will be there. I'm looking forward to meeting Nick Brown. I've heard so much about him. I feel bad about missing those rehearsals just before my first concert with the orchestra.'

'You couldn't help it,' Emma replied, glad that Paul hadn't said any more about Nick. 'John conducted and played the piano really well.'

'I knew he would.'

As Paul relaxed, slowly sipping his apple juice, Emma made final preparations for their meal. She put the roses in a vase and placed it in the middle of the table, then brought the food in from the kitchen.

'That smells wonderful. You've gone to a lot of trouble for me, Emma.'

'It was all quite simple,' she answered. 'I don't have the time or the energy to make anything too elaborate when I come home from school.'

'I'm sure it will be delicious,' Paul assured her. 'I'm sorry, Emma, I forgot to tell you how lovely you look tonight.'

'Thank you.' She could feel her heart racing and her face flushing.

They sat down and started eating. Emma told Paul about the last rehearsal, saying that they had all missed him and were concerned about his daughter. Then she found herself asking, 'Has Samantha phoned you this week?' As soon as the words were out, Emma regretted them. Why did she have to mention Sam again?

'No. Why should she? Although I believe she did ring the week before, but I was in too much of a state to reply. Perhaps I'd better call her to see what she wanted.'

I've done it again, Emma chided herself, *mentioning Sam. Now because of that, he's going to ring her. Why can't I keep quiet?* She quickly changed the subject. 'How old is Fleur?'

'She's six. I've loads of photographs of her at home. I'll show you another time.'

Emma thought elatedly, *There's going to be another time. Now I mustn't spoil things. I'd better not say anything about Fleur's mother tonight, but I do wish he'd tell me about her.*

When they'd finished eating, Paul offered to help Emma clear up, but she told him to leave it. 'You need a rest. Sit down and relax a few minutes before you have to drive home,' she urged. 'I can do it later.'

He sank back on the settee. 'If you're sure.'

'I am.' *He looks so tired*, Emma thought. For a few moments she saw the vulnerable man who so often hid behind an arrogant façade.

'You're spoiling me, Emma. Come and sit beside me, there's something I want to tell you.'

She sat down, wondering what he was about to say.

'About Fleur's mother . . . '

Emma felt pleased that at last he was going to confide in her. 'Yes?'

Before he could continue, the telephone rang. Paul groaned. *Why does it have to ring now?* she thought. 'I'd better answer it. I won't talk long. I'll get rid of whoever it is quickly.'

'Okay. You do that.' Paul leaned back and made himself comfortable against the cushions.

She picked up the receiver. 'Hello?'

'How are you, Emma?'

She nearly dropped the phone when she recognised Nick's voice. 'I wasn't expecting you to ring,' she replied, trying to steady her voice, noting that Paul was staring at her curiously.

'I've just arrived back in England. I told you in my letter, I was going to call. You did get it, didn't you?'

'Yes, but it's not convenient to talk now. I . . .'

Nick interrupted her. 'Oh Emma, it's lovely to hear your voice. I can't wait to see you again. Can I visit tomorrow evening? I'd like to come now, but I'm jet lagged and wouldn't be good company. There's so much I want to tell you, please say that I can come.'

'No, I'm sorry, you can't.'

'What do you mean? You've got a previous engagement?'

'Yes,' she lied, glancing at Paul who thankfully had closed his eyes.

'Well, I'll see you on Friday then. You will be at the rehearsal, won't you? I know you're a member of the orchestra now. We can talk afterwards. It's so good to be back. You're very quiet, Emma. You're not still mad with me, are you? I'll make it up to you. Everything will be fine again. I told you in my letter, I've grown up since I last saw you and I know what I want now.'

'I can't discuss this at the moment, I'm sorry.'

'Why? Have you got someone there?'

'No, I'm just very busy.' Another lie, she thought. Paul had opened his eyes and was looking at her.

'Don't hang up on me, Emma.'

'I've got to go.'

'All right. We'll talk on Friday, then. Goodnight. I'll be dreaming of you.'

She put the receiver down, feeling flushed and agitated. Why did Nick have to choose that moment to ring, just when everything was going so well with Paul?

'Are you all right?' Paul asked. 'You look hot and bothered.'

'I am,' she answered without thinking.

'Not bad news, I hope.'

'No, nothing like that. Don't worry. I'll get over it. Would you like a coffee?'

'Yes please.'

Emma was glad to escape to the kitchen. She leaned against the sink trying to steady herself. Why was life always so complicated? If only Nick hadn't come back. *It looks as if I'm going to have a difficult time trying to get rid of him*, she thought. *He's got the idea that we can start over again from where we left off. He doesn't seem to think that I might have found someone else. Whatever happens*

190

between Paul and me in the future, I want nothing more to do with Nick. I've got to make him realise that, some way or other.

Emma busied herself making the drinks. She put them and a plate of biscuits onto a tray and carried it into the lounge.

To her surprise, Paul was standing up, fastening his jacket, his face red and contorted with rage.

'What's wrong?' she asked with dismay.

'You've been leading me on. That's what's wrong,' he stormed. 'I'm leaving.'

'I've no idea what you're talking about.'

'Don't play the innocent with me.'

'I'm not. I really don't know what's made you so angry.' Emma tried to stay calm, but she felt close to tears. Paul's outburst was so unexpected. 'Look, sit down and tell me what I'm supposed to have done.'

'You don't know?'

'No.'

'When you were in the kitchen just now, the telephone rang again. I called to you, but you didn't hear, so I picked up the receiver.'

'Who was it?'

'That's what I would like to know.'

'Why? What do you mean?'

'Well, I guess it was the same person who rang a few minutes ago.'

'Oh no,' she murmured quietly.

'Oh yes.' Paul's voice was cold and hard, like his face.

'What did he say?' Emma whispered.

'I thought you'd want to know that,' Paul exploded. 'I was sitting here waiting, while your . . . your . . . your fancy man was chatting you up on the telephone . . . and . . . and you have the cheek to ask what he said.'

'Calm down, Paul. You've got it all wrong. Take your jacket off. Sit down and drink your coffee.'

'Don't tell me what to do.'

'I just want to explain everything. Please listen, Paul.' Emma tried to pacify him.

'It's too late for that. I've made a terrible mistake, trusting you,' he raged. 'What explanation can you give me? Are you going to tell me that you don't have a boyfriend?'

'I don't, Paul.'

'Well someone seems to think that you do, because he rang back to say that he'd forgotten to tell you that he loved you.'

10

Emma was very relieved when the bell rang for the end of school. The children had seemed particularly difficult to control and on several occasions she'd felt it necessary to raise her voice. Her friend Zoe had noticed Emma's downcast expression and enquired, 'Is everything all right? You don't look your normal cheerful self.'

'I'm not. I've no idea what's got into the kids today. They keep arguing with each other and they've done very little work. I'll be glad to go home. Thank goodness we haven't got one of our planning meetings tonight.'

Emma thought, *I'm lying again. I do know what was wrong. It was all my fault. I found it hard to concentrate and the children seemed to catch my mood, but I can't tell Zoe that. She'd ask too many questions and I don't want to talk to anybody about Paul. It's too painful.*

'My class were very unsettled too,' Zoe commiserated with Emma. 'That rain at playtime didn't help either. They'd just got into the playground when it poured, so they all came rushing in.'

'And after that nobody wanted to do any work,' Emma added.

'That's right,' Zoe agreed. You do look tired, Emma.'

'I am,' she replied. At least that was the truth. She'd slept badly. 'I think I'll have an early night and hope for a better day tomorrow.'

'I might do the same. Good night, Emma.'

★ ★ ★

That evening while Emma was soaking in the bath, thoughts of the night before came flooding back. If only Paul hadn't answered Nick's phone call everything would have been all right. It had been going so well up until then. She'd never for one moment imagined that Nick would ring. *He seems to have forgotten how badly he treated me and wants us to get back together as if nothing had ever happened. Even if Paul hadn't come on the scene, I wouldn't have gone back with Nick. I'll never forget how heartbroken I was when he went off with Chelsea, and yet he expects me to pick up with him as if the episode with her hadn't occurred. He says that he has grown up now and knows what he wants. Well, so have I, and I don't want him. The trouble is, Nick won't take 'no' for an answer, and now he's messed everything up between Paul and me, and I don't think that can ever be sorted.*

'What is going on?' Paul had demanded after Emma persuaded him to take off his jacket and sit down again.

'If you just calm down, I'll explain everything,' she'd said quietly, wanting to pacify him, but it didn't work. Instead they ended up having a blazing row. She'd tried in vain telling him that she didn't have a boyfriend, but he'd just shouted, 'Can't you tell me the truth for once?'

'Are you calling me a liar? You've got some nerve, Paul. You expect me to tell you every little detail of my life, but you conveniently forget to inform me that you have a daughter and . . . and . . . probably . . . a . . . a wife as well!' she'd screamed.

'We're not talking about me, we're — '

'There you go again,' Emma interrupted, 'turning things round. Everything has to be on your terms, Paul.'

'What do you mean?'

'You called me a liar, but you won't give me a chance to explain anything.'

'There isn't anything to explain. I thought I could trust you, but I've obviously got the wrong idea. You make friends with men very easily and don't seem to care whom you hurt in the process — Colin, Rob, and now this mystery man. Who is it, Emma? I know it wasn't Colin,' Paul taunted, as he marched across the room. 'I've enough problems with an orchestra to run as well as a book store to look after. I really haven't time for these squabbles. Thank you for my supper. I'll leave now, so you can ring your lover back.'

'Get out Paul,' Emma shrieked, flinging open the door, resisting the urge to push him, her eyes filling with tears of rage and frustration.

'Don't worry, I'm going.' He stomped off without another word and Emma slammed the door behind him.

She relived this scene over and over again in her head, wondering what else she could have said or done. *Paul's so unfair*, she told herself. *He didn't give me a chance to tell him about Nick and he's given me no explanation about his daughter and her mother. If Nick hadn't telephoned at that precise moment, everything might have been so different; Paul had been on the verge of talking about Fleur's mother. Now I'll never know. It's all over between us — not that it ever really got started,*

Emma reflected. Right from the beginning there'd been problems. *I've just got to forget Paul*, Emma decided. *There's no future for us*. At the back of her mind though, was the knowledge that she had to see Paul again at the rehearsals. That was going to be difficult, but she'd have to face it. The only alternative was to leave the orchestra, and she didn't want to do that. *I'm not going to let Paul have the satisfaction of driving me away*, she thought.

Emma stepped out of the bath, put on her peach dressing gown and settled down on the sofa to spend some time watching television, hoping that by staying up late to watch a film, it would help her sleep.

To her annoyance, the doorbell rang. *Now whoever can this be?* she wondered. *I'm not expecting anyone.* She peeped through the curtains and was horrified to see Nick standing outside. *Oh no, not him*, she gasped. Why did he have to come round? She pulled the curtains back quickly, but was too slow. She realised Nick had seen her.

'Emma,' he called.

She debated with herself whether to ignore him, but thought that might make matters worse. He rang the bell again more insistently, still calling her name. She went to the door, opened it slightly and said crossly, 'I told you not to come round.'

'Please let me in, Emma,' he begged, eyeing her up and down.

'No. It's not convenient.' She blushed, pulling her dressing gown tightly around her.

'Please, Emma. I need to talk to you.'

That was what Paul said, Emma mused, *and look how badly that ended*. 'But I don't need to talk to you,' she insisted, feeling even more embarrassed as she saw one of her neighbours walking past, giving them curious looks.

'I think you'd better let me in, otherwise all your neighbours will be wondering what you are doing, entertaining men on the landing in your dressing gown,' Nick smirked.

Emma quickly opened the door wider and he followed her inside.

'That's better. Now we can talk,' he asserted.

'I'll get dressed,' she told him. 'Go and sit in the lounge.'

'You don't have to get dressed on my account. You look fine as you are.'

'I won't be long.' Emma ignored him and hurried into her bedroom, firmly shutting the door behind her. A few minutes later she walked into the lounge wearing a grey skirt and top.

'That looks nice, but I preferred the dressing gown.'

'Nick! I don't want you here, and I certainly don't want to hear those kinds of remarks,' she said primly.

'I'm sorry. I'll try to be good,' he smiled.

'You've got a cheek coming here!' she exploded. 'What is there to talk about?'

'Well, before I start, there is one thing I want to know.'

'I want to know why you've come

here, even though I expressly told you not to,' Emma muttered, sitting down on the opposite side of the room.

'When I rang the second time yesterday,' Nick went on, 'you didn't answer but some man did.'

'So?'

'Who was it?'

'That's no concern of yours.'

'Yes it is.'

'No, it isn't. We're finished, Nick. I told you that.'

'I know you did, but I thought you were just mad with me and I'd be able to thaw you out.'

'You're wrong. That will never happen.'

'Don't say never, Emma.'

'You treated me very badly and I can't forget that.'

'But I'm really sorry for what I did. I shouldn't have gone off with Chelsea like that.'

'No, you shouldn't.'

'I regret it now. At the time I suppose I was infatuated with her and I felt flattered that she seemed so keen on me. She cast a spell over me, but I realise it was just a passing phase. The attraction soon wore off on both our parts. It's you I'm interested in, Emma.'

'In your letter, you told me that you only saw me as a sister.'

'I'm sorry,' Nick groaned. 'I don't know why I said that. My feelings towards you now certainly aren't those for a sister.' He got up from the sofa, went over to Emma, took her hand and begged. 'Can you ever forgive me?'

'No, I can't.' Emma pulled her hand away sharply.

'You haven't met someone else, have you?'

'I wouldn't tell you if I had!' she shouted. 'We're finished, Nick. Can't you understand that? I don't want any more to do with you. I wish you'd never come back.'

'Please don't say that. Is there anything I can do to make it up to you?'

'Yes. Leave me alone. That's all I want.'

'But Emma, I still love you. I . . . I . . . '

'You what?' How could he dare say that, after the way he'd treated her?

'I came here today to ask . . . ' Nick hesitated. 'To . . . to ask you to marry me.'

'You what?'

'I'm asking you to marry me, Emma.'

'Nick, you can't be serious.'

'I am. Please believe me. When I was in America, I had a lot of time to think about us and I realised what a terrible mistake I'd made.'

Emma couldn't believe what she was hearing. She hadn't expected this. She knew that Nick wanted to get back with her, but she'd been totally unaware of how serious he was. If he'd asked this question a few months ago, she would have been overjoyed, but now it was too late. She'd given her heart to someone else. She also realised that her feelings for Nick had never been as strong as those for Paul. It was the wrong man wanting to marry her, Emma mused. If

Paul had asked, even though she'd only known him a relatively short time, she would have gladly accepted. That would not happen now. Paul had called her a liar and walked out, because Nick had phoned at the wrong time. Life was so unfair. Hadn't Paul also said that?

'Are you listening to me, Emma? You've gone very quiet. Say something, please.'

'There's nothing to say.'

'You could agree to marry me. I'd be so happy.'

'But I wouldn't. No, Nick, I won't marry you.'

'Oh Emma, I'm so sorry I hurt you. In time you might be able to forgive me. We're so right together.' He tried to put his arm around her, but she dodged away.

'We wouldn't, because I know now that I don't love you.'

'What do you mean? Is there someone else?'

'That's no concern of yours.'

'I knew it. There *is* someone else.'

Nick's face became red. 'He was in the flat when I rang, wasn't he?'

'I'm not going to discuss it, but you can tell me something. What's happened to Chelsea? Why is she no longer the love of your life? Did she get tired of you, Nick?' Emma taunted.

'Don't be sarcastic, Emma. It doesn't suit you.'

'Don't you dare patronise me,' she snapped. 'Well, are you going to tell me about Chelsea? Did she find someone else?'

'Yes.'

'Someone her own age, I suppose.'

'How did you guess?'

'I thought as much. Oh Nick, how upsetting for you,' she mocked.

'Don't be so cruel, Emma.'

'Now you know how I felt when you went off with Chelsea.'

'I've said I'm sorry. What more can I do?'

'Nothing.'

'But Emma, I realise now that it was just an infatuation I felt for Chelsea. It's you I love. I've come to my senses. When I was asked to come back to England as the soloist with the orchestra, I thought that was my opportunity to make it up with you. I've been dreaming about it ever since. If you'd give me another chance I'm sure things could work out for us. We could both have a fresh start. I'm not only asking you to marry me, but also to move to America with me. You'd love it there. That's where my life is now. What do you say, Emma? Please say yes.'

11

'I'm waiting for an answer,' Nick said, taking hold of Emma's hand once again. 'Will you marry me?'

'I'm speechless,' she gasped.

'I'm sorry if I've shocked you. I . . . I . . . thought you'd be pleased.'

'No, I'm not pleased.'

'All right, you don't have to answer now. Perhaps I should have led up to this more slowly. Moving to America would be a big step for you, I know, but you'd like it there. I belong to an orchestra. I play percussion, keyboards, and sometimes piano solos. You could join it, too, now you've had the experience of playing with the Farwell Symphony Orchestra. John Grant told me you're doing very well.'

'You talked about me to him?' Emma was aghast.

'Why not?'

'What did you say?'

'We were just talking about the orchestra in general and he said that there were two new members as well as the conductor. What's the other chap like? He's called Colin, isn't he?'

'He's very nice.'

'Was it Colin who answered the phone?'

'No.'

'So who is the mystery man?'

'I told you, I don't want to talk about it.'

'Okay. Don't look so cross, Emma. I'll change the subject. John said the new conductor is very good. What do you think?'

'He is,' she answered quickly, not wanting to start discussing Paul with Nick.

'Well, as I was saying, you'd soon settle down in New York. Why don't you come and stay for the New Year holiday? I'm working in a university library. It's a great life, Emma. All I need now is for you to become my wife.' He moved closer again and put his arm around her waist, murmuring, 'I do love you.'

He attempted to kiss her. Emma pulled away and shouted, 'No, Nick! Stop it. I will never marry you. In time I might be able to forgive you for what you did and I will talk to you when I have to, but that's all. Is that clear?'

'Oh Emma, you're so hard on me.'

'Now you know how I felt when you were carrying on with Chelsea,' she said bitterly. 'I loved you then and I would have followed you anywhere, but that love died when you went to New York. I think you'd better go, Nick.'

'All right. I know when I'm beaten, but if you do change your mind, I'll be waiting for you.'

'I won't.' *I've had this conversation before*, Emma thought, *with Colin. Both Nick and Colin say they'll wait for me, but the one man I want has left me for good.*

Emma watched as Nick walked slowly and dejectedly along the landing, his shoulders hunched in misery. *He looks a different man from the one who entered my flat a short time ago, but at least he understands now, how I felt when he went off with Chelsea. I'm sure he'll soon get over it though. Perhaps in future he'll treat his women friends a little better.*

★   ★   ★

The next evening Emma was already seated beside Anthea at the rehearsal when Nick arrived. He was greeted enthusiastically by everyone. Bill introduced him to Colin and was about to bring him over to Emma, when Samantha walked in. She rushed up to Nick and threw her arms around him. 'It's lovely to see you again,' she said.

I had a lucky escape there, Emma thought.

'Sorry. I was going to introduce you to Nick,' Bill told her, 'but Sam got to him first.'

'It's okay, Bill. We have met.'

'Oh, I didn't know that.'

'Sam's really desperate for a man,' Anthea whispered to Emma. 'I suppose when Nick played with the orchestra before, she was going through her divorce, and didn't have much to do with him then.'

'Is she?' Emma replied, paying little attention to Anthea. She was trying to listen in to the conversation between Nick and Sam.

'What's Paul Kavanagh like?' he was asking Samantha. 'I gather he's not here yet.'

'A bit of a tyrant. Not like John.' She grimaced. 'He's often late.'

'That's not fair, Sam.' Anthea walked over to them and joined in. 'Paul's a good conductor but he's had a lot of problems.'

'Yes. A daughter being one of them,' Sam answered sarcastically.

'I seem to have missed a lot,' Nick smiled. 'How's your husband, Sam?'

'Oh, of course you don't know. I'm divorced now, and a good thing too.'

'I'm sorry, Sam.'

'Don't be. Life's a lot better without him.'

'I've missed more than I realised,' Nick told her.

'I'll fill you in on all the details at coffee time,' Samantha promised.

They're getting on well together, Emma thought. *Maybe she'll leave Paul alone and switch her affections to Nick and take him off my hands.*

A few minutes later, Sam decided to take charge of the orchestra. 'Now, everybody, I think you should tune your instruments, so that when John and Paul arrive we are all ready to start.'

There was a hubbub of noise as they took their places and began tuning. Nick sat down at the piano and watched. Emma couldn't help noticing that he kept looking in Samantha's direction. *I think he's getting interested in her already. He's so fickle! Last night he was swearing undying love to me. Now because I rejected him, he's turning his attention on Sam. Well, she can have him.*

Anthea had been observing them too. 'Sam's in fine form tonight,' she whispered to Emma. 'She's certainly giving Nick the eye. Well, I suppose he is very good-looking. She seems to have got over Paul already.'

Before Emma could think of a reply, John came in with Paul striding behind.

'How's your daughter?' several people asked.

'Getting better, thank you, was his brief reply.

Soon they were all immersed in the music. Paul was pleased with the standard they had reached. 'I think our first concert together will be a great success,' he told them.

'That's praise indeed,' Bill remarked to Anthea.

When the interval came, Samantha, Nick, Paul and John sat chatting to each other, while Emma stayed with Anthea, Bill and Colin. The second half passed uneventfully, everyone working hard to make their concert a success. Emma was feeling very relieved that there hadn't been any embarrassing scenes with Nick. She hurried home afterwards without saying a word to him or Paul.

During the next week, Emma heard nothing from Nick, Paul or Colin. She spent her evenings alone. *That's how it's going to be from now onwards*, she told herself, *so I'd better get used to it. I've rejected Nick and Colin and Paul has finished with me.*

★   ★   ★

The day of the concert arrived at last. All the members of the orchestra had been eagerly anticipating this. Emma made up her face carefully, put on her long black chiffon skirt and white blouse. She was feeling very nervous, but at the same time excited. She arrived early at the hall and was pleased to see that Anthea and Colin were already there.

'You two ladies look lovely,' Colin remarked, smiling broadly.

'Well, you look very smart yourself,' Anthea told him.

'I'm not used to these clothes. I feel a bit too dressed up.'

'They suit you,' she assured him.

'I've got terrible butterflies,' Colin added.

'So have I,' Emma joined in.

'Stop worrying, you two. It will be fine.'

'I hope you're right,' Colin replied.

The hall was unusually full, since word had got around that there was a new conductor with the orchestra, and people wanted to see what he was like. Also, many remembered Nick and had come along to see him once again.

As Paul stepped onto the dais with his usual arrogant swagger, Emma thought that he looked magnificent in his black evening jacket and white frilled shirt. She couldn't take her eyes off him, but he didn't even glance in her direction. She guessed that he, too, must be feeling nervous as this was his first performance with the orchestra, but there was no evidence of this as he raised his baton ready to begin conducting.

Silence immediately descended on the hall as the opening bars of Beethoven's 'Egmont Overture' were heard. Once Emma started playing she became immersed in the performance, her tumultuous emotions finding a natural outlet in the music. As each work was finished, Paul inspired the orchestra ever onward to greater things, until the climax came with Nicholas Brown's rendering of Grieg's 'Piano Concerto'. Nick, too, looked magnificent; Emma couldn't deny that. Both men were such a contrast to each other, Nick so fair and Paul so dark.

Nick was in excellent form that evening and received a standing ovation at the end of the concerto. The audience were reluctant to go home and kept cheering until Nick, in consultation with Paul, gave an encore and played a couple of piano solos, a Chopin prelude and the 'Revolutionary Study'. A reporter from the local newspaper was there and several photographs were taken of Nick, Paul and the orchestra. Emma felt thrilled to be part of this scene and was glad that she had joined the orchestra. She was also pleased with her own performance and relieved that she hadn't let anyone down by making careless mistakes. Her practice had paid off. She just wished that her personal life had been equally satisfactory.

Emma's friend Zoe was at the concert. Afterwards she came to speak to Emma. 'That was wonderful. Nick Brown's a brilliant pianist and your new conductor is fabulous. You didn't tell me about him,' she said reproachfully.

'Didn't I?' Emma answered, thinking, *Now Zoe's falling for him too.*

'Come on, everyone,' John called to the members of the orchestra. 'It's party time.'

'I've got to go,' Emma told Zoe. 'I'll

see you at school on Monday.'

They all made their way to the room where they practised on a Friday evening. Some of the older ladies who no longer worked had made it look very festive. There was a long table laid with a delicious-looking buffet supper.

One of the younger members had been put in charge of the music and had chosen a selection suitable for all tastes and age groups — ballroom, disco and line dancing.

Colin asked Emma for the first dance, a waltz. 'It all went very well tonight,' he commented. 'I'm so glad I joined the orchestra. Aren't you?'

'Yes,' she replied, thinking, *I would be if it wasn't for my problems with Nick and Paul.*

'You dance beautifully, Emma,' Colin told her. 'I'm not very good. My feet don't do what I want them to. I find disco dancing much easier.'

'Don't worry about it.' Emma smiled. 'You've done a lot better than some of the others. They really haven't got a clue.'

Colin glanced over to where Anthea was struggling to teach Bill how to waltz. 'Poor Anthea,' Colin whispered. 'She looks quite exasperated.'

'I don't think dancing's Bill's scene, but at least he's trying,' Emma added.

At the end of the dance they sat down next to the older couple. 'I'm exhausted after that,' Bill remarked. 'I need a rest. I'm sorry, Anthea, but I don't think I'll be doing many more dances this evening. I'm getting too old for so much exercise.'

'That's all right, Bill. It's a line dance next. Will you join in with me, Emma?'

As the two women walked onto the floor, Anthea whispered, 'Bill's hopeless. He's no idea where to put his feet. I'll be quite relieved if he does sit out for the rest of the evening.'

When that was finished, Emma sat down and chatted to Colin. She watched as Nick danced with Samantha, who looked as if she was enjoying herself, smiling and talking in a very animated way. Emma had also noticed that Paul had been taking turns dancing with some of the older ladies in the orchestra. When she saw him heading towards her group, Emma got up and persuaded Colin to join in the next disco dance with her.

'I'd love to,' he replied.

She was sitting down trying to catch her breath afterwards when Nick approached. 'Will you dance with me, please, Emma?'

Reluctantly, she agreed. She didn't want to make a scene and draw attention to herself in any way.

'You look lovely tonight,' Nick told her.

'And you played beautifully. I've never heard you play so well.'

'It must be because I poured out all my pent up emotion into the music. I still can't believe that you've ditched me.'

'As I've said before, now you know how I felt.'

'I'm sorry, Emma, I really am.'

'You'll get over it, Nick.' Then she couldn't resist saying, 'Samantha will help you.'

'Do you think so?'

'I'm sure she will. She's very impressed with your playing.'

'Perhaps I'll ask her for another dance.'

'You do that.'

Out of the corner of her eye, Emma observed that Paul was now dancing with Anthea. When she noticed him looking across at her, she quickly glanced away and continued talking to Nick. 'Samantha's a very good violinist,' she remarked.

'Yes, she is,' he replied. 'Paul Kavanagh's done a good job with the orchestra too. I like his passionate style of conducting, but he seems a bit of a sombre person.'

'Well, his daughter has been very ill.' Emma found herself defending Paul.

'So Samantha was saying.'

When the dance ended, Emma sat

down and Colin fetched her a drink. 'Thanks, I needed that. I think I'll sit out for a bit. I'm like Bill, not used to all this exercise.' She smiled. 'You go and dance with some of the others, Colin.'

'If you're sure you don't mind.'

'Not at all. I might get myself something to eat. I'm feeling rather peckish. I'll enjoy watching for a while.'

Emma helped herself to some of the refreshments and sat down at a table. A couple of the older members of the orchestra came up to her. 'All on your own, dear? Can we sit with you? It's a good evening, isn't it?' the elderly lady said. 'Where's your young man gone?'

'I haven't got a young man.'

'Oh, I thought you were going out with Colin.'

'No, we're just friends.'

'Oh, that's a shame. Still, he shouldn't have left you on your own.'

'I don't mind. I wanted a rest.'

Emma ate her food and watched everyone around her. They all looked happy and relaxed. She noticed that Paul was dancing with Anthea again, and was surprised at how good he was. Then she told herself she shouldn't have been, because Paul was the sort of person who did everything well. She was also aware that Samantha and Nick had spent the last few dances together. She was gazing up at him in open admiration and he seemed to be delighting in all the attention he was getting. Colin, too, looked as if he were enjoying himself with some of the other young people. Everyone seems so contented. *Except me*, Emma thought mournfully. *I should be happy. I've achieved my ambition of getting into the orchestra. I've a good job, lots of friends, but I haven't got a man in my life and the one I want hasn't even spoken to me this evening. I have to forget him*, she told herself. *He's in the past. Now, I must make a new life for myself.*

Emma was gazing around the hall, lost in thought, when she was startled by a familiar deep voice saying, 'I think it's time I had a dance with you.'

Immediately her heart started to race, but she replied, 'Oh Paul, do you really want to?'

'I've asked you, haven't I?' he snapped, his blue eyes glinting. 'Don't play hard to get, Emma. It's not your style. Just have this one with me. I'm trying to dance with all the lady members of the orchestra, so don't spoil my plans.'

'I wouldn't dream of doing that,' she replied sarcastically. 'I mustn't thwart the great and mighty Paul Kavanagh.'

'You're forgetting where we are, Emma,' he stated imperiously, taking hold of her arm and leading her onto the dance floor. 'This is supposed to be a party. It's not the place to continue our altercation.'

She flushed, feeling like a schoolgirl who'd been told off by her teacher. They danced in silence until Paul remarked, 'Feeling upset that Nick's not dancing with you?'

'Why should I be?'

'Well, it was him that phoned you the other evening, wasn't it?'

'How do you know?'

'I have my ways of finding out.'

'Been checking up on me, then?'

'Don't be coy with me, Emma. You're not the little innocent you pretend to be.'

'You . . . you . . . '

'Now, now. No temper tantrums here, please. Remember where we are.' He gripped her arm tightly.

She wanted to slap his face, but had to restrain herself. This was not the place to make a scene. Paul was right about that. She glanced around the hall to see if anyone was looking at them, and noticed Sam deep in conversation with Nick. 'I couldn't dance with Nick if I wanted to,' she blurted out. 'Samantha is monopolising him.'

'Ah Samantha,' Paul murmured. 'She seems to cause you a lot of trouble.'

Immediately Emma regretted mentioning Sam. Now Paul would think that she was jealous of her. Why did she always say the wrong things to Paul?

'You're right though,' he continued as the music came to an end. 'Sam is monopolising Nick. I'll have to put a stop to that. If you'll excuse me, Emma, I'll go and have the next dance with her.'

As Emma walked over to a seat, she saw Paul approach Samantha. She couldn't hear what was being said, but Sam was smiling up at him, looking much happier than of late.

I've done it again, Emma thought, *driven Paul to Sam. I can't seem to help it.*

Suddenly a voice enquired, 'All on your own?' Nick sat down beside her. 'I saw you dancing with our conductor.'

'Yes. I'm having a rest now.'

'Perhaps we could have another dance together?'

'In a minute. Let me get my breath back first.'

They sat watching the couples on the floor. Emma couldn't help thinking what a fine pair Paul and Samantha made. They were both excellent dancers. She wondered if she'd forgiven him for not telling her about his daughter. 'You've spent a lot of time with Sam tonight,' Emma stated.

'Are you jealous?'

'Of course not.' She wished she hadn't made that remark.

'She's a good dancer. I didn't know about her divorce until the other evening. I remember her ex-husband, a rather pompous man. I always wondered why she married him. He used to come to our concerts occasionally. Anthea told me that he left Sam and went off with someone else. Sam's so attractive, I can't imagine why he'd want to do that. She seems to have got over it very well though,' Nick observed.

Emma had the next dance with Nick. After that, she danced with some of the other members of the orchestra but didn't speak to Paul or Nick again. She noticed, however, that they seemed to be vying for Samantha's attention. Emma wondered if Sam was trying to make Paul jealous by monopolising Nick — or was it the other way round, that she was spending time with Paul in order to make Nick envious?

John Grant danced with Emma and told her he was delighted with her progress. 'You settled down very quickly with the orchestra and have done so well.'

Emma was pleased at his kind words but felt they were rather exaggerated. She was convinced that Paul wouldn't agree with that statement, but didn't say this to John. After all, Paul was in charge, but he'd offered her few words of encouragement.

That night Emma arrived home with ambivalent feelings. She was thrilled that the concert had gone so well, and thankful for John's praise. She was also glad that there had been no embarrassing episodes with Nick, but her disastrous encounter with Paul had left her feeling extremely upset. She knew now without a doubt that there would be no reconciliation between them, but that knowledge only made her more miserable. If only she could get him out of her system.

* * *

The few weeks leading up to Christmas seemed to pass quickly. John, Bill and two other members of the orchestra came to Emma's school and gave a recital to the children, which was enjoyed enormously. Emma joined in on her violin for some of the items, to the delight of her class.

The orchestra started work on John's new rhapsody and also prepared for the carol concert. Paul was a hard taskmaster and Emma found she had to do a lot of practice to keep up.

Colin asked Emma to go out with him once again but when she refused, he didn't press the matter.

Nick returned to America after agreeing to come back to England in the summer to be their soloist for Rachmaninov's 'Second Piano Concerto'. 'That's something I've always wanted to play,' he told everyone. 'I'll need to start work on it straight away. It's not going to be easy.'

'I'm sure you'll manage,' John told him.

Emma heard no more from Nick and was relieved that at last he seemed to have taken the hint and was leaving her alone. She wondered whether he would keep in touch with Samantha. Nothing was ever said about it at rehearsals in her presence.

Paul also had made no effort to revive their friendship. Emma was glad that her schoolwork kept her occupied, otherwise she might have felt lonely. She knew it was all her own fault. She had handled everything so badly. She'd ruined any chance she ever had with Paul by making stupid thoughtless remarks. She knew that if she wanted, Colin would jump at the chance of going out with her, but that wouldn't be fair to him, when her thoughts were centred on another man. The only social life she had now was each Friday attending the rehearsals, where she sat chatting to Anthea and Bill, who seemed to be getting on very well with each other, making Emma feel that she was an intruder. When she mentioned this to Anthea one evening, she told her not to be so silly. 'Bill and I are just good friends. That's all.'

Emma was not so sure if that was the truth.

At each rehearsal, Emma noticed that Paul and Samantha seemed to be back on their old friendly footing.

'I think they're together again,' Anthea whispered one evening.

'It looks like it,' Bill confirmed. 'I heard Sam telling Rose, who sits next to her, that she had met Paul's daughter. She said her name's Fleur and she's gorgeous, with huge blue eyes and lovely long brown curly hair. She said she's the image of Paul.'

'You heard a lot.' Anthea smiled.

'You know me. I like to find out what's going on, so I keep my ears and eyes open.'

'Yes, I know you very well,' Anthea laughed.

'So, maybe Paul hasn't got a wife after all,' Bill added. 'Perhaps he is a widower. Anyway, he seems to have sorted things out with Sam.'

Emma's heart sank. *Samantha must be going out with Paul. And she's met his daughter too. I finally drove them together. I'll have to get used to it, but I wish he still didn't have this devastating effect on me. Since that night when Paul came round and Nick phoned, I've spoken very little to Paul, yet whenever I see him, I can feel my pulse racing, even though most of the time he either ignores me or is icy polite.*

★　★　★

Emma broke up from school for the Christmas holiday the day before the carol concert. She was planning to spend most of the time with her family, returning early in the new year. Colin had invited her to go to a party with him on the first of January. Emma was relieved that she had a genuine excuse for refusing his invitation.

'When you get back, perhaps we could go somewhere then?' Colin suggested. 'I know you don't want to get involved with me, but it seems silly for both of us to be on our own. Couldn't we just go out as friends? No strings.'

'I'll think about it,' Emma promised. *After all*, she thought, *what have I got to lose? I'm lonely; so is Colin. There's no harm in us just being friends, as long as he keeps to that.*

★   ★   ★

The day of the concert saw the first snow of the season. Everywhere was clothed in a white blanket. Farwell was an attractive town at any time of year. All its residents and shopkeepers decorated every available space with numerous flower beds, window boxes and hanging baskets full of flowers. It looked particularly lovely when the trees and surrounding fields were covered in snow.

Emma had been looking forward to the carol concert. She loved choral music, especially Handel's 'Messiah', some of which they were performing with the choir from Farwell Parish Church. John Grant who was their organist had agreed to play for a few of the carols, so that the members of the orchestra could join in with the singing.

The church was a very large nineteenth-century building with a lofty ceiling and a balcony spanning three sides, providing space for several hundred people. Despite the snow, every seat in the church soon became occupied on the night of the concert and extra chairs had to be placed in the aisles. The orchestra and choir were arranged on staging in the chancel. Emma had arrived early and was sitting next to Anthea, watching people coming in. She saw Paul enter with a smart middle-aged woman, who was holding the hand of a little girl wearing a blue coat and matching boots. He ushered them to seats at the front of the church. They both had dark hair like Paul's; the woman was very attractive and the child extremely pretty. *So that must be Paul's mother and daughter*, Emma thought. The child gave Paul a hug and a kiss before sitting down beside her grandmother. Paul beamed at her, waved, and marched up onto the platform, where he was busily arranging various sheets of music and papers ready for the carol concert to begin.

Emma still had no idea whether Paul was divorced, widowed or had an ex-partner. She found it hard to believe that any mother could leave such a gorgeous little girl, so she concluded that Paul was a widower. How sad it must be for the child, she mused.

Soon Handel's music was filling the

church. Emma had to concentrate on her playing and put all thoughts about Paul and his daughter out of her mind. During the second half of the concert, Emma enjoyed herself singing the carols as John's performance at the organ echoed around the building.

'John's a good organist,' Emma whispered to Anthea.

'Yes, he is. Have you seen Paul's daughter?' the older woman asked. 'She's been sitting perfectly still throughout the concert. What a demure, well behaved little girl.'

'That's what I was thinking,' Emma replied. 'I wish the children in my class were half as good.'

At end of the concert, the vicar invited everyone there to attend the morning service the next day. Afterwards, people were talking outside the church and some were discussing whether to go or not. Emma decided that she would have time to go before getting packed up to visit her parents. Colin said that he might attend too, but

Bill declined the invitation. 'My church-going days are over,' he muttered.

'Shame on you, Bill.' Anthea smiled. 'It might do you good. I was thinking of going along myself. I was hoping you might join me.'

'In that case, how can I refuse? I'll see you there,' Bill laughed.

Emma was half listening to the conversation, but at the same time watching Paul from a distance as he was speaking to his mother and daughter. She saw him kiss both of them and wave as they walked towards the car park. She then noticed Paul striding over to Samantha and John Grant, who had just come out of the church.

'I'd better go now,' Emma told Colin and Anthea. 'I've lots to do. I'll probably see you all in the morning.'

'I'll walk you to your car,' Colin said.

'There's really no need,' she told him. 'I'll be quite safe. There are lots of people around. You stay and talk to the others.'

'If you're sure you'll be all right.'

'I'm certain. Good night. See you tomorrow.'

Emma hurried to the car park. She opened the car door and was just about to get in when someone shouted, 'Be careful! You just missed me.'

Her heart skipped a beat when she looked up and saw Paul standing in front of her. 'You're dangerous with a car, Emma. This is the second time you've nearly hit me.'

So, he *did* remember meeting her in the car park all those months ago, Emma thought. She had often wondered about that. 'Oh, sorry. I didn't see you,' she replied.

'No. You never do. Look, Emma, it's almost Christmas. We haven't spoken properly for weeks.'

'And whose fault is that?' she retorted.

'All right. It's mine.' Paul held his hands up. 'I'm trying to apologise. Please don't start arguing with me again. I'm sorry I was so rude to you

239

that night in your flat when you received that telephone call from Nick. I don't know what came over me, but Emma, we can't leave things as they are over Christmas. Do you think you can ever forgive me?'

12

Emma was astonished that Paul had apologised to her. This was the last thing she had been expecting, believing that any relationship she'd had with him was over. She realised that for such a proud, arrogant man, saying sorry was not an easy option, but nevertheless, she was delighted that he had sought her out to do so.

'Yes, Paul, of course I'll forgive you,' Emma replied without hesitation.

'You will?' He sounded incredulous. 'I said some very unkind things and I didn't give you a chance to explain anything. I'm afraid I tend to jump to conclusions and react before I find out what the truth is.'

'I'm just the same,' Emma confided. 'I speak without thinking too.'

'And don't I know it!' Paul grinned. 'You've withered me with your tongue on many occasions.'

'So, we're equal now.' Emma smiled.

'And we can start all over again?'

'Yes, Paul.' She couldn't believe this was happening.

He touched her hand. 'You're freezing. I'm sorry to keep you out here in the snow, but I couldn't let things go on any longer as they were. I had to apologise before Christmas.'

'I'm well wrapped up. Besides, it's a lovely evening. I've never seen so many stars at this time of year. Look at that one over there, shining out. It makes you think of the Christmas story and the star that was shining over the stable.'

'You're right. It is a beautiful evening,' he murmured. Then, changing the subject, asked, 'I suppose you'll be staying with your family for Christmas?'

'Yes, I leave on Monday morning.'

'I was hoping I could have seen you before then. There's lots we need to talk about.'

'I second that,' Emma breathed. 'Like

telling me what's happened to your wife.'

'Oh, is that bothering you? I have no wife. I'm divorced. But you haven't told me about Nick.'

'We can't talk here, Paul.'

'You're right. Besides, I can see you're shivering.' He sounded concerned. 'I don't want to make you ill for Christmas. You've already had the flu once this year.'

'And anyway, the others are coming out of the hall now,' Emma added.

Paul looked round and groaned as he saw Anthea and Bill heading towards them. 'Why can I never get you to myself? Will you ring me as soon as you return to Farwell? Please, Emma?' he mouthed. 'If I'm out you can leave a message and I'll get back to you.'

'I will,' she promised. 'Or Paul, I could give you . . . '

She didn't get a chance to finish, as Bill and Anthea stood in front of them. She'd been about to ask Paul if he wanted her mobile phone number. Then he could have contacted her sooner.

'Still here, Emma?' Bill remarked. 'We thought you'd be home by now.'

'It's my fault. I nearly collided with her,' Paul answered gallantly. 'And I kept her talking in the cold.'

'It was a good concert tonight,' Bill commented. 'The vicar's delighted. He's discussing it with John now. He wants to see you, Paul, to arrange something for Easter.'

'Let's get Christmas out of the way first,' Anthea laughed.

'I'd better go and find the vicar then,' Paul replied. 'Well, I wish you all a happy Christmas.'

'Aren't you coming to the service tomorrow?' Bill asked.

'No. I would have done, but we're attending St. Luke's Church in Lynsford. It's their nativity play and Fleur's an angel, so I can't miss that.'

'Of course you can't. How lovely! I hope it goes well. Has she fully recovered yet? She's a sweet little thing,' Anthea added.

'Yes, she's quite well, thank you. In fact, back to her old self. It was pretty frightening at the time though, when she was in hospital, not knowing what was wrong and if she'd ever get over it.'

'It must have been,' Anthea sympathised.

'Goodnight everyone,' Paul called as he strode off towards the hall.

'Happy Christmas,' they chorused.

Emma watched as he approached the hall. She noticed that Samantha and Colin were standing outside, chatting. She saw Sam grab Paul's arm, whisper something in his ear, and then kiss him on the cheek.

'Did you see that?' Bill whistled. 'Sam's just kissed our distinguished conductor.'

'She kissed Colin too,' Anthea added.

'Sam's certainly full of Christmas spirit,' Bill replied. 'Good night, Emma. We'll see you in the morning. Come on, Anthea. Time to go.' He took her arm possessively and led her across the car park.

Emma drove home in a much happier frame of mind than when she'd arrived at the hall. Paul wanted to see her again. This thought was going round and round in her head. He'd asked for her forgiveness and he'd cleared up one mystery. He'd told her that he was divorced, but now she wanted to know the details.

Emma wondered about the kiss Paul had received from Samantha, and what his reaction was. Did he return the kiss later? Sam was a friendly person, Emma rationalised. She'd done the same to Colin. It was probably just her way and meant nothing special. But then, when she remembered Sam's boast of meeting Paul's daughter, she ended up in a state of confusion. *One minute I'm overjoyed that Paul wants to see me again, and the next I'm worrying about Samantha and her relationship with him.*

* * *

On Monday, Emma travelled by train to visit her family. The snow that had looked so attractive in Farwell had turned to slush in London. It was cold and dreary outside and Emma was glad to get into the warmth of her parent's home.

'Go into the lounge,' her mother ordered, after greeting her daughter.

Emma did so and found her grandmother sitting on the settee. 'How lovely to see you, Gran,' she said, hugging and kissing her. 'And you look so well.'

'I'm fine, dear. Really on the mend now.'

'How long have you been out of hospital?'

'Two days. Your dad brought me home.'

'She's been a good girl doing her physiotherapy.' He winked.

'Now, Emma, you come and sit beside me and tell me all about what you've been doing,' Gran urged.

Emma told her about school, the orchestra, the carol concert, and the Christmas service she'd been to the previous day with most of the other members of the Farwell Orchestra. She didn't mention anything about Paul, however. She would wait and see how that relationship developed before telling any of her family about him.

On Christmas Eve, Emma's brother Ben arrived with his girlfriend. 'We're spending Christmas here and New Year's with Karen's family,' he informed her.

Emma was delighted to meet Karen at last. She thought that her brother's description had, on this occasion, been totally accurate. Karen was a very attractive young woman with long blonde hair and enormous brown eyes.

The family all had a happy time on Christmas Day, exchanging presents and eating too much. Gran was very lively, thoroughly enjoying herself. Emma was amazed to see this, remembering how only a few weeks ago she'd feared that her grandmother wouldn't survive until Christmas.

'Don't forget your promise to give me a violin recital before you go back to your flat,' Gran reminded her.

'No, I won't do that.' Emma smiled. 'I struggled home on the train with my violin, so I'm going to make sure you listen to me practising.'

On Boxing Day they had a special party to celebrate Gran's ninetieth birthday, which had been in November when she'd been so ill. Lots of friends and relations gathered round and they all had a marvellous reunion.

★   ★   ★

The time soon came for Emma to return to Farwell. She was sad about leaving her family, but looking forward to seeing her friends again, especially Paul. She debated with herself whether to phone him as soon as she got back or wait until the next day.

Emma was all packed up ready to go, eating lunch with her parents and grandmother, when the telephone rang. Her mother answered it and after a brief conversation rushed back into the dining room, her face flushed with excitement.

'What's up?' Emma's father enquired.

'You'll never guess!' she shrieked.

'Tell us, dear,' Gran said. 'It must be something interesting. You look quite pink.'

'I can't believe it.'

'Helen, what can't you believe?' her husband asked.

'It's Ben. He's got engaged to Karen. We're going to be parents-in-law!'

'Ooh how lovely,' Gran exclaimed.

'Ben told me it was the real thing with Karen, but I didn't take any notice, he'd said it so many times before,' Emma laughed.

'I hope he knows what he's doing. They're both so young,' her father stated.

'They're not getting married for a

couple of years as Ben's still at College,' Helen told them.

Emma was pleased at the news, but surprised to think that her little brother was engaged already! She quickly rang to congratulate him.

★ ★ ★

On her journey back to Farwell, Emma decided to contact Paul that night. She wondered what sort of Christmas and New Year he'd had. She also contemplated her relationship with him. Would it develop in the next few weeks or would it just fizzle out? What about Samantha? Was she still on the scene?

Then there was the mystery of Paul's marriage and his daughter. Why was Fleur living with Paul and not with her mother? So many questions! Would she ever find out the answers?

That evening Emma dialled Paul's number, eagerly waiting to hear his voice, but she was disappointed. His mother answered and told her that he wasn't in. 'You're a member of his orchestra, aren't you? I'll tell him you rang, but he won't be in till late. He's gone out with friends. I said I'd look after Fleur, so he could have some fun.'

'That's kind of you,' Emma replied.

'Well, Paul works much too hard. He puts in long hours at the store, and then in the evening he's busy studying the music scores.'

Emma thought, I should have realised that. It's not only the members of the orchestra who have to spend a lot of time practising, but the conductor has to know the music in great detail too.

'I've no idea where Paul went,' Mrs. Kavanagh continued. 'Samantha arranged it, so I expect they'll be having a good time. You know what she's like. The life and soul of the party!'

'Yes, I do,' Emma murmured.

★ ★ ★

On Saturday, Emma woke up feeling tired after a restless night. She'd been tossing and turning thinking about Paul and Samantha on their night out with some friends. There were so many questions she wanted answered. Where did they go? What had they been doing? Did they stay in a group, or did they pair off? Was Paul interested in Emma, or was it really Samantha he wanted? How did Paul's mother know that Sam was the life and soul of the party? Had she met her? If so, when? Had Paul taken her to his house?

Emma kept herself busy getting ready for her return to school on Monday, but all the time listening out for the sound of the telephone. She hoped that Paul's mother would remember to tell him that she had called and that he would ring her back. Her patience was rewarded in the afternoon. After briefly discussing their Christmas and New Year's celebrations, Emma couldn't resist asking, 'Did you enjoy your evening out?'

'Yes, very much thank you. It made a

change. I was sorry to miss your call, though.'

'I believe Samantha arranged the evening for you.'

'That's right. There were ten of us from the orchestra, mostly the younger ones. We had a meal and then we danced. It's ages since I've done anything like that, apart from the night we had the party for Nicholas Brown. It was great fun.'

'Oh, I bet Samantha enjoyed that,' Emma blurted out without thinking.

'Yes. We all did actually, but I didn't ring up to talk about Samantha.' His voice sounded stern.

'Oh,' was all Emma could think of to say. Why did she have to put her foot in it and mention Sam once again?

'What I rang up for, was to ask if you were doing anything tonight,' Paul continued.

'No.'

'Good. Maybe we can have dinner together? It's time we did some talking. What do you say, Emma?'

'That would be very nice,' she replied, her heart leaping for joy. She was so glad that she hadn't got a previous engagement. 'What about Fleur though?'

'My mother will be delighted to look after her. The two of them love spending time together. I'll pick you up at seven then. Is that all right?'

'Yes, fine.'

That evening Emma took great care with her appearance. She had on a short black straight skirt, a silver glittery evening top and black patent high heels. Over this, she wore a grey imitation fur jacket.

I mustn't ruin everything tonight, she kept telling herself. *I've got to keep my tongue in check. It's a long time since our first date and a lot has happened. I've got to be very careful about what I say, otherwise this might be our very last date!*

As usual, Paul arrived exactly on time, looking immaculate in his dark suit. 'You look lovely,' he murmured.

'Thank you. Where are we going? I

wasn't sure whether this outfit would be suitable.'

'It's just perfect. I've booked a table at a restaurant in Lynsford, not far from where I live.'

'I've never been there.'

'Lynsford's pleasant enough. Quiet. Not too big, and pretty in the summer.'

A few minutes later they parked the car outside the restaurant. It was at the end of a row of shops, small and exclusive-looking. As they entered, the manager greeted them effusively. *What a fabulous place*, Emma thought, noticing how elegant everyone looked. Soon they were enjoying their meal. The waiter was discreet but attentive. Conversation flowed freely, although nothing of a personal nature was discussed. Emma didn't want to spoil the pleasant atmosphere by asking questions, so instead they talked about the orchestra, her school and other topical subjects.

When she'd finished eating, Emma sighed and remarked, 'If I ate many meals like that, I'd need to buy a whole new wardrobe of clothes. Nothing would fit me. I'm glad I let you choose from the menu. You have such good taste.'

'Thank you for the compliment. I'm glad you aren't a fussy eater. You really enjoy your food, unlike some women who pick at everything, worrying about their diets.'

'And you've taken out so many,' Emma said impulsively, immediately regretting it.

'Well, why shouldn't I?' Paul challenged. 'I am human, you know. I'm thirty-five and I'm not a monk.'

'No, I know you're not. Monks don't usually have daughters.'

'Are you going to hold that against me?'

'Of course not,' Emma answered quickly.

'I made a big mistake with my marriage.' Paul sounded bitter. 'Have I got to pay for that for the rest of my life?'

'I'm sorry. I didn't mean to offend you. It's just my stupid tongue. I told you, I always speak before I think.'

'All right. Apology accepted. When I mentioned women and their diets, I was actually thinking about my ex-wife. She was always worried about her figure and half-starved herself as a consequence.'

Emma kept quiet. Was Paul going to tell her about his wife at last?

'Fleur was the only good thing to come out of the marriage,' he continued. 'But I don't want to talk about that tonight. Thinking about it will only ruin the atmosphere.' Then, changing the subject, he said, 'If you've finished your coffee, Emma, and it's not too cold for you, we could have a walk around Lynsford. I know it's dark, but I'll show you the main street and the river.'

'I'd like that,' she replied. 'And I need the exercise.'

They strolled along beside the river, the water shimmering in the moonlight. They chatted companionably. Emma was thinking how well the evening was going, apart from one little misunderstanding. It was so much better than their previous date. She didn't want anything to spoil it. She was still curious about Paul's marriage, but she'd have to wait until he was ready to discuss it with her.

'Would you like to meet Fleur and my mother?' he was asking.

Emma hadn't expected this. 'I'd love to,' she replied. 'Samantha says she's very sweet.'

'Samantha! Why have you brought her up again?'

'I shouldn't have said that.' Emma was annoyed with herself.

'You seem to be obsessed with her,' Paul stormed.

'Aren't you?' Emma retorted, glancing up at his face. She wished she'd kept quiet when she saw how angry he looked. *Why do I say these things?* she asked herself.

'I am not, repeat, *not* obsessed with Samantha,' Paul stated, quickening his pace so Emma was forced to speed hers up too, which wasn't easy in her high-heeled shoes.

'Have you told Sam about your wife?' Emma really wanted to know the answer to this question. 'You're reluctant to tell me about her, for some reason,' she continued.

'That's because it's all in the past. We're divorced. Finished. Can't you understand that?'

'Is that what you told Sam?' Emma couldn't stop herself now. She had to get it out of her system.

'What has my wife got to do with Samantha?' Paul sounded exasperated.

'I . . . I don't know.' She seemed unable to refrain from making these remarks, adding, 'I suppose Sam's met your mother?'

'Stop, Emma. We're doing it again. Arguing.' He stood and faced her.

'Well, it's not my fault,' she muttered stubbornly, looking at the ground.

'It never is,' he replied sarcastically. 'But to answer your question, yes, Sam has met my mother. She's known Sam for years. Since she joined the orchestra, in fact.'

'Oh.' Emma was beginning to feel rather foolish.

Paul went on, 'My mother goes to most of their concerts. She used to go with my father. He was a friend of John Grant and after their concerts they would often all have a drink together. I'd forgotten that, but my mother reminded me of it the other day when I said I was going out with some of the members of the orchestra.'

'I see,' Emma murmured.

'Good. I hope you do. Let's continue our walk.'

'Can we go a bit slower?'

'Sorry, I forgot you were wearing those heels. Now, can I tell you one more time? I have no interest in Samantha whatsoever, apart from as a friend and a fellow musician. She is too much like my ex-wife. Will that convince you?'

'Yes Paul, but does Sam know that?'

'I hope so. Samantha is a very good violinist and I've been discussing with her whether she'd be willing to play the violin solo in Vaughan Williams' 'Lark Ascending'.'

'Oh, I understand now. I tend to jump to conclusions too quickly.' Emma's voice was low and apologetic.

'Yes, you do.' Paul continued, 'Sam really makes the violin sing and plays so expressively, that I thought she would be able to cope with the part. She was very reluctant about it at first, feeling she wasn't good enough, but I think I've persuaded her to do it at our summer concert.'

Emma felt sorry that she'd spoiled the tranquil atmosphere, but glad that some matters had been resolved at last. Before she could think of a reply, Paul added, 'Sam met my daughter one Sunday afternoon, when I called round to give her the music. I was on my way to the park with Fleur. Does that satisfy you?'

'Yes. I'm sorry, Paul.'

'It's time we cleared the air once and for all. Of course I was flattered by Samantha's attention. Any man would be. We both have the same sense of humour and she's very attractive, but once she found out about Fleur, she lost interest in me. She doesn't like children.'

'I didn't know that.'

'There's a lot you don't know.'

'Well, tell me then.'

'I suppose I went along with Sam's flirting because I was annoyed with you, thinking that you were getting involved with Colin. Perhaps I wasn't fair to Sam, but I think she's quite capable of taking care of herself.'

Paul stopped, turned to Emma, took hold of both her hands and asked, 'Now do you understand?'

'I think so,' she breathed.

'What about Colin and Nick? It's time you told me about them.'

'As I've said before, Colin is just a friend and Nick is someone from the past.'

'All right Emma, that will do for now. We've had enough explanations for one evening.' He released her hands and they continued walking. 'I hope you like Fleur. I think she's a delightful child, quite grown up for her age, but of course, I am biased.'

'She's very pretty.'

'She looks like her mother.'

'I can't wait to meet her.'

'My mother dotes on Fleur. Treats her like the daughter she never had. Why don't you come round one day after school? My mother will provide a meal.'

As Paul drove Emma back to Farwell, she was feeling relieved that apart from the tricky patches, when Samantha was mentioned, everything had gone much more smoothly than before. Best of all was the fact that Paul wanted to see her again. He escorted her up the stairs to her flat and said, 'Emma I . . . I . . . ' He hesitated.

'What is it?'

'I think it would be best if we didn't

mention to any members of the orchestra that we are . . . er . . . seeing each other.'

'If that's what you want,' Emma agreed, but she had mixed feelings about this. She liked the sound of 'we are seeing each other', but had reservations about keeping it secret. She was so excited that she wanted to tell everyone, but she could see Paul's point of view. It was early days yet and anything could still happen. Hadn't she felt the same way, not wanting to mention Paul to her family, in case anything had gone wrong?

'Yes please, Emma.'

They made arrangements for her visit and then Paul lightly brushed his lips against her cheek and hurried away.

13

Emma returned to school in a happy frame of mind on Monday for their staff training day. Zoe enquired if she'd had a good Christmas.

'Yes, thank you. It was lovely,' she replied, thinking, *And this week might be even better when I see Paul again.*

On Wednesday Emma was in a highly nervous state, as it was that evening she was due to visit Paul and his mother and daughter. She kept telling herself not to be silly. *You teach children all day and have no problems getting on with them, so why are you concerned about meeting Fleur?* Emma still had a niggling worry about Paul's reticence in letting other members of the orchestra know they were going out together. Was it because he thought it might only be a passing phase and would soon be over? Or did he genuinely want to wait and see how things developed, before telling anyone? She hoped it was the latter.

Emma had decided to wear a smart black skirt with a cheerful red sweater for her visit to Paul's home, knowing that children liked bright colours. As she opened the front door for him, he kissed her lightly on the cheek and said, 'You look nice.'

'Have you had a good day?' she asked.

'Not really. There were some awkward customers who wouldn't be pacified by my manager, and insisted on seeing me. I had to use all my tact and patience to sort them out and there was so much paperwork to do, I had to leave a lot of it otherwise I would have been late in collecting you. But that's enough about work. Let's go.'

Twenty minutes later they arrived at Paul's house. It was situated on the outskirts of Lynsford. Emma hadn't known what to expect, but she had never imagined that his house would be so huge. It was about a hundred years old, detached, set well back from the road with a slate roof, a long drive and an attractive well-cared-for garden. 'What a lovely house,' she gasped. 'It's a . . . a stately home.'

'Not quite.' Paul smiled. 'It belonged to my grandparents and they passed it on to my mother and father.'

Now that the moment had come when Emma had to meet Fleur and Mrs. Kavanagh, she was feeling beside herself with nerves. His family were obviously very wealthy and Emma felt out of her depth. *They won't like me*, she feared. *I'm too ordinary*. Then she wondered whether Paul's wife had got on with his mother. Had there been some problems between the two, which had led to Paul and her splitting up? Was Mrs. Kavanagh a difficult woman?

Paul parked the car outside and led Emma to the front door. He placed his key in the lock and they entered a large square hall with a galleried stairway and landing. All the walls were adorned with portraits which Emma guessed were of his family.

'I'm home,' Paul called.

Fleur came running into the hall, slamming a door behind her as she shrieked, 'Daddy, look at my new dress! Do you like it? Grandma bought it for me after school.'

'It's lovely,' Paul answered as he picked her up and swung her around. 'Fleur, this is Emma. She's going to have tea with us today.'

'Oh, hello. Grandma said you were coming. We've got iced cakes. Jenny made them.'

'Jenny comes in to help my mother with the work,' Paul explained. 'This house is too much for one person.'

'Hello, Fleur. I love your new dress. It's really pretty.'

'So are you. Just like that lady we went to see . . . you know, Daddy . . . the one with long hair.'

'Yes, dear,' Paul answered.

'I know what her name is,' Fleur continued. 'It's Sam, isn't it?'

'That's right. We took her some

music, didn't we?'

'Yes, and she gave me some choco-
lates. They were yummy.'

Emma noticed that Paul had lost his
self-assured air. In fact, he appeared
quite embarrassed. *I seem to be
haunted by Samantha*, she thought.

Emma seized the opportunity to
change the subject by opening her bag
and taking out the gift she had bought.
'This is for you, Fleur. If you've got it
already, I'll change it for a different
one.'

'What is it?' she squealed, ripping the
wrapping paper and pulling out a book.
She stared at the cover. 'It's got a cat on
it. I love cats. I'm good at reading. *Six
Dinner Sid*,' she said, sounding out
each letter. 'That's funny.'

'Fleur definitely hasn't got that one,'
Paul told Emma. 'It sounds intriguing.'

'It's a lovely story. At least I think it
is. I'll read it to you later, Fleur, before
you go to bed, if you want,' Emma
promised.

'Thanks,' Paul whispered, looking

relieved that the tricky situation had passed.

Fleur grabbed hold of Emma's hand and begged, 'Come and see Kitty. Can we, Daddy?'

'Everyone who comes here has to be introduced to Kitty.' Paul winked at Emma.

'Kitty's your cat?' Emma guessed.

'How did you know?' Fleur looked impressed.

'Yes you two, go and find the cat. I'll see what Grandma's up to.'

'She's getting tea ready,' Fleur confided. 'Come on, Emma.'

She led her up the staircase to one of the rooms off the landing. It was large and bright, decorated in pink, and full of toys, cupboards and bookshelves. At one end was a bed with frilly covers and matching curtains hung at the windows. A typical little girl's room, Emma thought. She'd have loved one like that when she was a child, but times were hard then and Emma's room had been quite basic, not luxurious like this one.

Emma decided that Paul's mother must have designed it. She couldn't imagine Paul playing any part in something so feminine.

Fleur let go of Emma's hand and ran over to the sofa, where a ginger cat was curled up, sleeping.

'Kitty, wake up. Someone's come to see you.' She shook the cat.

'Don't disturb her. I can see how beautiful she is.' The cat opened her eyes, yawned and then settled down again. 'She's quite big,' Emma said as she gently stroked her, while the cat purred contentedly.

'Grandma thinks she's too fat. Daddy says she's a rare cat. Do you know why?'

'No. You tell me.'

'Because she's ginger. Most ginger cats are boys. Didn't you know that?' Fleur was scornful.

'No. I've never had a pet cat.'

'Don't you like animals? I love them.'

'Yes, I do like animals, but when I was a little girl my brother had asthma.

272

He was allergic to cats. Do you know what that means?'

'You keep sneezing.'

'That's right. My brother would cough and sneeze if he got close to any cat fur, so we couldn't have any pets.'

'What about dogs? You could have had a puppy.'

'I'm not sure. My mum wouldn't let us have any pets in case it made my brother ill.'

Before they could continue the conversation, Paul walked into the room with his mother, a tall, dark-haired, well-dressed woman. She greeted Emma warmly, saying, 'I've spoken to you a few times on the telephone. I'm very pleased to meet you at last. You're a teacher, aren't you?'

'Yes, at Farwell Primary School.'

'I remember my husband talking about you,' she said wistfully. 'Hubert used to come home from Kavanagh's and say he'd been speaking to a nice young teacher from the primary school.

I think it must have been you.'

'He was a very kind man, so helpful,' Emma answered. 'Always ready for a chat with his customers. He often helped me find a book I needed for school.'

'You're right. We miss Hubert so much. It's terrible without him, isn't it, Paul?'

'It is,' he replied, his face shadowed. 'But we didn't bring Emma here to talk about our troubles.'

'I miss Granddad too.' Fleur joined in the conversation.

'I know you do, sweetie.' Paul's mother hugged her. 'But you've got us.'

Soon they were sitting in the dining room, eating sandwiches, sausage rolls, fancy cakes, fruit salad, jelly and ice cream. Emma relaxed, enjoying herself. Fleur was a friendly little girl. Emma was amazed at how well adjusted she was, considering the upheavals she must have had in her short life. She wondered how long it was since Paul's divorce, and if Fleur ever saw her mother now. And why did Paul have custody of his daughter, instead of his ex-wife?

Mrs. Kavanagh was very welcoming and easy to talk to. Paul, too, showed a different side to his character. He was no longer arrogant, but attentive towards Emma and his mother and very affectionate with his daughter. Seeing Paul in this situation made Emma's heart overflow with love for him. They were all getting on so well together. The silly arguments they'd had seemed a thing of the past. Emma wished it could always be like this. She'd managed to keep quiet even when Fleur had mentioned Samantha. Why couldn't she do this when she and Paul were alone together?

At eight o'clock, Paul told Fleur it was bedtime. She was disinclined to leave them all, but when Emma reminded her that she would read *Six Dinner Sid*, she capitulated gracefully.

Afterwards, the three adults sat in the elegant and spacious lounge around a log fire, chatting and listening to light classical music. Emma felt completely at ease and very content. Everything had gone so much better than she'd hoped.

There were a lot of photographs displayed around the room, mostly of Fleur and a couple of Paul and his parents, but there were none of his brother or of his wife. Emma wondered why but didn't like to ask.

At one end of the room was a grand piano. 'Do you play the piano?' she enquired of Paul.

'Yes, and Fleur is having lessons as well. The piano belonged to my grandmother, my father's mother. She was a good pianist and very knowledge-able about music. It was she who inspired me to have a musical career.'

'Paul's a good pianist too,' Mrs. Kavanagh told Emma.

'But I don't get enough time to practice these days,' he answered.

★　★　★

276

When it was time to leave, Emma felt astonished that she had fitted in so well with Paul and his family. In spite of their wealthy appearance, they were quite ordinary and unpretentious. Mrs. Kavanagh, like Fleur, begged Emma to come again soon, and she said that she'd be delighted to, if Paul asked her.

'Of course I want you to,' he answered. 'You must know that, Emma.'

She thought, *I don't know that. In fact, I have no idea what Paul really thinks.*

They were both quiet on the journey back to Farwell, but Emma felt it was an amicable silence. She was pondering how Paul's wife could have borne leaving such a delightful child as Fleur. Why was she being brought up by her father instead of her mother?

Emma glanced at Paul from time to time. He too looked relaxed and happy, so different from his appearance when Hubert had been mentioned. Then, his face had been grim and brooding. *He's taken his father's death very hard*, she thought.

On their arrival back at Emma's flat, she said, 'Thank you, Paul, for a wonderful evening.'

'Did you really enjoy it?'

'Yes. Fleur's lovely and your mother is so kind and friendly.'

'I'm glad you liked them. It's important to me that you all get on well together. Do you think we could go out for dinner on Saturday? It's time I gave you some explanations.'

'That would be very nice.'

Paul put his arms around Emma, kissing her lightly on her cheek. Then he looked into her eyes and kissed her lips very gently, gradually becoming more passionate. She responded as if in a dream. Was this really happening? She'd waited so long, and now Paul was kissing her as if he really cared. Suddenly he released her, saying, 'I'm sorry, I got carried away.'

'Don't be sorry, Paul.'

'You mean you're not annoyed with me?'

'No, of course not.' She reached up and kissed him.

A few moments later, Paul strode off and Emma almost bounced into her flat, she was so happy. *This has been one of the best days in my life*, she thought. *At last I've seen the real man behind the stiff and starchy façade which Paul shows to other people.*

★ ★ ★

The next day at school, Emma went round in a daze of happiness. All she could think of was that Paul had kissed her as if he meant it, and she was going to have dinner with him on Saturday, and he intended to give her some answers to her questions. Life was marvellous, she felt, and it showed on her face.

On Friday evening when Emma arrived for the first orchestra practice of the year, Anthea was already there, tuning her violin. 'I'm glad you've come early,' she said. 'There's something I want to tell you.'

'What's that?'

'Samantha telephoned me the other day and asked about you and Nick.'

'What did she want to know?'

'She said that she thought you used to go out with Nick and wondered if you were still in touch with him.'

'What did you reply?'

'The truth. That I didn't know what was going on, and anyway it wasn't my business.'

'Thanks, Anthea. I wonder how Samantha found out that I used to go out with Nick. It all finished a long time ago and I'm not in the least bit interested in what he does now.'

'That sounds very definite.'

'It is.' Emma thought, *Sam's gone straight from Paul to Nick. She seems desperate for another man in her life and doesn't seem to care who it is. She can have Nick as far as I'm concerned.*

'Sounds as if you've got your sights

set on someone else. Is that it?' the older woman asked.

Emma was spared from answering as Bill came in and walked straight up to Anthea and placed a kiss on her cheek.

'Oh Bill,' she protested feebly.

Emma laughed and continued tuning her violin.

'Where's Sam?' Bill whispered.

'Must be working late again, I suppose,' Anthea replied.

Paul climbed onto the platform, sorted his music, tapped his baton for silence, smiled and said, 'Good evening, everyone. Happy New Year.' He looked round until his eyes rested on Emma.

She smiled back at him, her heart beating erratically. Then she became aware that Colin was gazing at her, so she waved to him and mouthed, 'Hello.'

Paul raised his baton to start conducting. Suddenly their peace was shattered by the sound of the door crashing open. Samantha once again made a dramatic entrance, tripping across the hall in her three-inch, stilettos. 'Sorry I'm late. I got held up at work. Can you wait a minute please, while I tune my violin?'

'You have five minutes,' Paul told her. 'Then we really must get started. We have a lot to do.'

'Hurry up, Sam,' someone called. 'You mustn't keep our conductor waiting.' Everyone laughed as she tottered dramatically to her place, nearly falling over on the way. *Samantha still loves being the centre of attention*, Emma thought. She was surprised to see that Paul was smiling too. *He really seems to have mellowed a lot recently.*

During the break, Paul sat with John. Emma guessed they were discussing the music, as they were flicking through their copies of John's new composition.

Samantha left them alone and came over to Emma, Colin, Anthea and Bill, who were drinking coffee together. 'Guess who I've had a letter from?' she said.

'I don't know,' Colin answered. 'You tell us.'

'Nick Brown. He's going to ring me another day from America.'

I knew she was going to say that, Emma thought, *but I'm not bothered by it.*

'How is he?' Colin asked politely.

'Very well. He's actually playing a solo with an orchestra in New York next month.'

Emma was aware that Samantha was watching her. *She wants to see what my reaction is to her news*, she thought, *but I'm going to keep quiet.*

Bill answered, 'Nick's the best pianist we've ever had with the orchestra. He'll go far.'

They finished their drinks and were walking back to their places when Paul beckoned Emma across to him. 'Is it still on for tomorrow?' he whispered.

'Why shouldn't it be?' Emma enquired.

'No reason, except that I can't believe how lucky I am.'

'I'm the lucky one,' she breathed.

Emma sat down, but Bill had noticed Paul talking to her. 'Are you in trouble?' he joked. 'Have you done something wrong?'

'Shush, Bill, leave her alone,' Anthea urged.

'Everything's fine,' Emma reassured him.

'You know, Paul's looking remarkably cheerful tonight. I wonder why he's so happy. Samantha's paid him little attention, so it's nothing to do with her. He must have found himself someone else,' Bill quipped.

'I wonder,' Anthea replied, smiling at Emma.

When the rehearsal had finished, all the members of the orchestra were very enthusiastic about John's rhapsody and he was satisfied with Paul's conducting. 'You've got it sounding just the way I wanted it. I couldn't have done better myself.'

'It will be the climax of our concert in February. I think it's going to prove a very popular work,' Paul told him.

'Each part blends so well together, making a beautiful, rich, romantic sound.'

'Here, here.' As usual, Bill had been listening in to their conversation and took the opportunity to join in. 'It's brilliant, John.' He applauded as he stood chatting to them.

Emma agreed. She'd practised hard during the Christmas holiday, as had most of the other members of the orchestra. She was thinking that although she and Colin were the newest recruits, everyone had made them very welcome, and now they felt quite at home. She remembered how she'd nearly left the orchestra, believing that Paul had noticed all the mistakes she'd made. How long ago that seemed now, and what a lot had happened since then! She was so glad that she'd persevered with her practice and stayed with the orchestra.

They were packing up, ready to go home, when Anthea remarked, 'Do you remember when you came to see me and I told you about Bill?'

'Yes.' Emma waited.

'We . . . we've reached a compromise. I think I said that love could grow out of friendship.'

'I remember.'

'Well, it has.'

'Oh Anthea, I'm so pleased for you.' Emma hugged her. 'I suspected something tonight when he came in and kissed you.'

'You know what Bill's like.' She smiled. 'He's over the moon. I've agreed to see him three or four times a week, although I won't live with him yet. I value my independence too much at the moment. We'll see how it goes from there. Bill seems quite satisfied with that. I think we'll have the best of both worlds. We've actually arranged to go on holiday together at Easter.'

'That's lovely. I hope you'll both be very happy. You're just right for each other. Everyone thinks so.'

'Do they?'

'Well, the people I've spoken to do.'

'What about you, Emma? Have you got anything to tell me?'

'Not yet.'

Bill came over to them, put his arm around Anthea protectively and asked, 'What's she been saying?'

Emma looked at the older woman, who nodded encouragingly. 'Anthea's been telling me about your little agreement.'

'Good. Now that she's made it public, she'll have to keep to it.' He kissed her on the cheek.

'Oh Bill,' Anthea sighed.

They're like a couple of lovebirds, Emma thought.

'What's going on here?' Colin enquired with a grin. He'd packed his music away and had come over to see Emma.

'Anthea's consented to be my lady friend,' Bill answered proudly. 'I'm so lucky.'

That's what Paul said, because I'm having dinner with him tomorrow, Emma mused.

'Congratulations.' Colin shook Bill's

hand. Then he turned to Emma. 'Can I escort you to your car? It's time we had a chat. I haven't seen you on your own for ages.'

She wondered what he had to say, but couldn't think of any excuse to get out of it. 'Yes, all right,' she replied.

Emma called 'Good night' to everyone and was following Colin out of the door when she noticed Paul watching her. *Why did he have to see me leaving at the same time as Colin? I hope he won't be annoyed about it. I couldn't have refused though. It would have looked churlish.*

As they stopped beside Emma's Mini, Colin blurted out, 'Is something going on between you and Paul?'

'What makes you think that?' she prevaricated, shocked at his question. Did she and Paul look different somehow? Emma had a feeling that Anthea was suspicious too.

'I saw you together tonight, smiling and talking very cosily. Then I remembered Paul coming to your flat after the fire.' Colin's face was grim.

'Do I have to ask your permission before I smile or talk to anyone?' she blustered.

'No, of course not. I'm sorry, Emma. I didn't mean to offend you. It's just that I care about you and I don't want you to be hurt.'

'You don't have to be concerned about me. I can look after myself.'

'Not always. What about the night of the barn dance?'

'Do you have to remind me?' she groaned.

'Sorry, Emma.'

'Oh all right. You came to my rescue that night and I was very grateful for it, but most of the time I am quite capable of looking after myself.'

'I hope so, but if you do ever need me . . . if things don't work out . . . I'll be there waiting for you,' Colin assured her.

'Please, don't. Find someone else. I'm not right for you.'

'But you are, Emma.'

'No, Colin.'

'I'll never feel the same way about any other woman.'

'Never is a long time. You might change your mind later,' Emma told him as she got into her car.

'I don't think so,' he replied. 'But I'll say no more now. Good night, Emma. I hope you won't get hurt by . . . by Paul.'

Emma drove home feeling sorry for Colin, knowing that his love for her was hopeless, but she was powerless to make him see that. She wondered if she should have denied being involved with Paul, but this would have meant telling a lie and she didn't want to do that. The fact that she hadn't denied it must have confirmed Colin's suspicions. She hoped he wouldn't tell anybody about her and Paul just yet.

* * *

The next evening, Emma was ready when Paul came to collect her. As she opened the door, he kissed her and commented favourably on her appearance, but said no more until they were driving along in his Mercedes. Emma guessed what was bothering him, but was determined not to mention it unless he did.

After a few minutes, the question came. 'What did Colin want last night?'

'He was just being thoughtful, escorting me to my car, making sure I was safe. After all, you didn't offer.'

'You know why. People would have noticed.'

She felt like replying, 'They have already,' but instead said, 'Is that so terrible?' Emma was getting worked up. 'Are you ashamed of going out with me? Am I so far beneath the great Paul Kavanagh?'

'No, of course not. You know it's not that. How could you even think it?'

'What is it, then?' she snapped.

'It's just . . . that . . . it's early days yet. We don't want everyone talking until we're more sure of each other.'

'So, you still don't trust me?' *Here we go again*, Emma thought. *Will we ever stop arguing?* 'You seem determined to think the worst of me.'

They were driving along a quiet country lane. Paul stopped the car, pulled over to the kerb and unfastened his seat belt.

'What have you done that for?' she shouted.

'Because I can't concentrate on driving when you start screaming at me.' He took hold of her hands firmly.

'I'm not screaming. I'm trying to make you see how unreasonable you're being.' She wriggled free.

'Me, unreasonable! You're the most exasperating woman I've ever met. One minute, you're all quiet, shy and demure, and the next you're ranting and raving at me like a demented tigress.'

'And you're so . . . so . . . pompous, arrogant and . . . ' Emma never finished the sentence. Paul deftly undid her seat belt, put his arms around her and gave her a long, lingering kiss. He stopped, held her away from him for a moment and gazed into her eyes, but she reached up and kissed him. When they'd finished their passionate embrace, Emma whispered breathlessly, 'Aren't we supposed to be on our way to a restaurant?'

'Yes, but I've waited so long to do that.' He released her. 'Okay, let's get going.'

They fastened their seat belts. Before Paul re-started the car, he said, 'Look, Emma, the main reason I don't want you to tell anybody about us is, I'm worried that when I've told you everything, you might not want to continue going out with me.'

14

Whatever is Paul going to say? Emma thought. Nothing could be bad enough for her to want to finish with him. 'I'm sure it won't make any difference to me, no matter what you have to tell me,' she replied.

'If only I could believe that,' Paul sighed.

Thirty minutes later they were in the heart of a small village, a few miles outside of Farwell, seated in an elegant restaurant, eating a delicious starter which Paul had selected with his usual impeccable good taste.

Emma didn't want any more disagreements to spoil the evening, so she decided to try and reassure Paul about Colin. 'You know I've told you there's nothing going on between me and Colin and never has been?'

Paul nodded.

'Well, the truth is, he would like us to be more than friends, but I don't feel that way about him. Do you believe me?'

'Yes, Emma. And do you believe that nothing's going on between me and Samantha?'

'I do. Besides, I think she's got her sights set on Nick now and she's welcome to him.'

'You haven't told me what happened with him yet.'

'No, but I will if you promise to tell me about your wife.'

'It's a deal. But I'm worried what your reaction will be when I tell you everything about my family.'

'I'm sure you don't have to be.' Emma tried again to reassure Paul, but he still looked anxious. What was he going to reveal about his family? Why did he think it would make her want to finish with him?

As they ate their meal, Emma told him about her broken relationship with Nick. Paul listened patiently and sympathetically, holding her hand across the table when he observed that parts of the story still upset her.

When she'd finished, he remarked, 'It's no wonder you didn't want Nick to come back here. He treated you so badly, running off to America with Chelsea like that, and then returning to England expecting you to resume your relationship with him. He does seem insensitive!'

'That's what I think. Anyway, that's enough about my problems,' Emma said.

Before Paul could say anything else, the waitress brought them their coffees, remarking, 'What a terrible night. It's streaming down. I hope you've got your umbrellas, or you'll get soaked going to your car.'

'I hadn't realised it was raining. We've been so engrossed in our conversation. That puts paid to any walks tonight, Emma. We'll sit here for a while. Maybe it will have stopped by the time we've finished our drinks,' Paul replied.

'I hope so,' the waitress answered. 'I've got to get home in it too. It's really dreadful now. Take your time with your coffee. We won't close for ages. No one will leave yet. It's too bad.'

When the waitress had walked away, Paul took hold of Emma's hand again and said, 'I've been wallowing in self-pity for what my wife did, when all the time you've suffered the same thing with Nick. I'm so sorry, Emma.'

'Now it's your turn to talk,' she replied.

'It's not a pretty story.'

She squeezed his hand. 'First of all, before you tell me about your wife, can you explain how you came to be the conductor of Farwell Symphony Orchestra?'

'Well, as you know, I was a lecturer in music. I worked and lived in London. I used to conduct the university orchestra and the choir. I loved the work even though my personal life was not happy. I had always intended to have a musical career, from a very early age, playing the piano and the clarinet and singing in choirs.'

'I didn't know you played the clarinet,' Emma interrupted. 'Were you a tenor? I love listening to opera. There are so many brilliant arias written for the tenor voice. You'll have to sing to me some time.'

Paul laughed. 'Don't get carried away. I was a baritone, not a tenor.'

'I should have guessed,' Emma smiled, 'with your deep voice. Anyway, sorry for the interruption. Please carry on.'

'About two years ago,' Paul continued, 'I had decided to change my job and leave London. I wanted to move near to my parents' home in Lynsford. My marriage was over. I was left on my own to bring up Fleur. My parents were more than willing to help. I was in the process of applying for another lecture-ship, when by chance, John Grant was at one of the concerts where I was conducting. He came to speak to me afterwards and said that he would be retiring from the Farwell Symphony Orchestra within a couple of years, and thought that I might be a suitable candidate to succeed him.'

'I wondered how you knew him,' Emma joined in.

'I don't know him very well at all, but he's certainly helped me out. I owe him a lot. He eventually recommended me to the panel of interviewers for the orchestra and I was successful. But to go back to my story, John speaking to me like that gave me another incentive to move to Lynsford. I was fortunate in securing a lecturing job closer to my parents' house and I rented a flat just outside the town.'

'It must have been hard bringing up Fleur without your wife, even though you had the help of your parents,' Emma remarked.

'It was. I had a succession of nannies, but whenever they left it was upsetting for Fleur.' Paul's face was dark and brooding as he continued. 'After . . . after my father died . . . ' he sighed, stopped speaking and put his head in his hands.

Emma tapped him gently on the shoulder. 'What happened Paul?'

He straightened up, pulled himself together and went on, 'My mother suggested that I move in with her. She would have company and be able to help me out with Fleur.'

'That sounds like a good idea.'

'It's worked very well and has given Fleur a lot more security.'

'And your wife, Paul? What happened to her?'

'Lucinda . . . she left me and Fleur to go and live with . . . Dave, one of the other lecturers at the university in London. Someone who I thought was my friend. I'd no idea what was going on. We hadn't been happy together for a long time, but I hadn't suspected that.'

'Oh Paul, that's terrible. I'm so sorry. It must have been awful for you.' Emma clasped his hands, wanting to comfort him. 'I thought Nick treated me badly, but what Lucinda did was so much worse. Poor little Fleur.'

'Fortunately she was too young to understand. Lucinda had never been a proper mother. Since Fleur was born I've had to provide her with enough love for both of us. You see, my wife didn't want children. She thought it was a dreadful mistake when she became pregnant. I hoped that after the baby was born, she would see things differently, but she didn't. She seemed completely devoid of any mothering instinct.'

'How did you come to marry Lucinda?' Emma was trying to comprehend how any woman could reject her own child as well as her husband.

'We met at a friend's party, ten years ago. She was the most beautiful woman I had ever seen, and I fell for her in a big way. I'd been so busy following my musical career that I'd had little time for getting involved with anyone, and she dazzled me. We were married within eighteen months and at first were very happy, but things changed when she became pregnant. She blamed me, saying she wanted to continue working and didn't want to be a mother.'

'What was her work?'

'She was a buyer for a fashion company, which meant that she often had to go away from our house in London. After the birth, Lucinda went back to work as soon as she could. We both earned enough money to employ nannies to take care of Fleur and I was able to work from home some of the time, which helped. Right from the beginning, Lucinda showed scant love for her child, so when we separated and finally divorced, she was happy for me to have custody of Fleur.'

'It's difficult to believe a mother could be so unconcerned about her child,' Emma interrupted.

'In her case, it would have been better if she hadn't become a mother. Children were just a nuisance as far as she was concerned.'

'Poor Fleur.'

'She's actually coped well. You can't

miss what you've never had. To Fleur, Lucinda was just a pretty lady who occasionally fondled and made a fuss of her when she felt like it, and when she didn't, expected others to care for her child.'

'So when did you split up?'

'Lucinda was always going off, leaving me to look after Fleur. I thought she was away on business a lot of the time, but one day we had an almighty row and she said that she was tired of playing the doting mother and wanted more from life than that. Then she confessed that she was having an affair with Dave and was going to move in with him. I couldn't believe it at first and pleaded with her to stay for Fleur's sake, but she wouldn't listen, and went upstairs and started packing her things. Amazingly, Fleur slept through all of this and by the time she awoke the next morning, her mother had gone.'

'Thank you for telling me, Paul,' Emma said, reaching across the table and kissing him.

'I'm afraid there's more yet.'

'Your brother? You haven't told me about him.'

'That's not easy to tell.'

'Do you want to talk about it another time?'

'No. I've got to do it now. I can't leave it any longer. I'm just worried about your reaction.'

'You don't have to be. Nothing can be that bad.' Emma took his hands in hers, trying to reassure him.

'It can. My brother, Chris . . . he . . . he's in prison. There, I've said it. Oh Emma, you look so shocked. I knew you would be, but I felt I had to tell you. It wouldn't have been fair to keep it from you.' His eyes were dark with anguish. 'Now you know the truth, do you still want to see me?'

'Oh Paul, whatever your brother's done, it makes no difference to me. You're not responsible for him.' Emma squeezed his hands. He'd been right. She was shocked. She would never have guessed that his brother was in prison, but in no way did she hold it against Paul. She had to find a way of making him understand that.

'If only I could believe that,' he replied.

'You must, otherwise I'll be accusing you of calling me a liar, and we don't want to start all our rows over again do we?' Emma smiled at Paul, trying to lighten the situation.

'I can't believe you're taking this so well.' He was staring at her in astonishment.

'Look Paul, I'm going out with you, not your brother, so whatever he has done doesn't concern me. Do you want to talk about it?'

'Yes. I've got to get it over with now.'

'So what did he do?'

'Chris was a gambler. He was addicted to it and got himself into a lot of debt. He was always asking me to lend him money. I did some of the time, but I realised that this wasn't really helping him, so I refused. Then we discovered that he'd been taking money from the bookstore, just small amounts at first.' Paul paused and took a deep breath. 'My father was in a terrible state and didn't know what to do. We both tried talking to Chris, but he wouldn't listen. I even suggested he join Gamblers Anonymous, but it fell on deaf ears. My brother had always been stubborn, thinking that he knew best. He told us that he would beat the addiction in his own time and way, but of course he couldn't.'

'Oh, Paul. It must have been awful for you and your parents.' Emma's eyes filled with tears of sympathy. 'So what happened?'

'Chris started taking larger amounts of money, until my father felt he had no choice but to report it to the police. It . . . it . . . ' Paul gulped. 'It broke his heart to do so, but he thought it was the only way to stop Chris. The police came and arrested him. He was taken to court and eventually sentenced to eighteen months in prison. He should be out in another six months. My father was never the same after that. It affected his health. He suddenly looked an old man, although he was only sixty-five. It was probably the stress which caused his . . . his . . . ' Paul's voice wavered, 'his fatal heart attack.'

'What a terrible story! I'm so sorry, Paul. You must have been devastated. And all that time, as well as worrying about your brother, you had your problems with Lucinda to cope with and a little daughter to bring up. It makes my troubles seem very petty in comparison. Does Chris have a wife?'

'No, fortunately. He couldn't settle down. He had a succession of girl-friends, but no one really serious, and once he got into gambling in a big way, they all deserted him.'

'So Chris should have taken over Kavanagh's Bookstore when your father died?' Emma was trying to puzzle everything out.

'Yes. He'd been the manager of a large bookshop in London. He'd run it very successfully until gambling took over his life. Then he left his job and came back home. My dad tried to get him involved in the business, hoping it would break his habit, but by then it was too late. Dad gave Chris an ultimatum. He told him to get treatment for his addiction. If he didn't do this, he would have to give up his right to inherit Kavanagh's and also his share of my parents' house.'

'What did Chris say?'

'He said that he couldn't promise to do that. My dad was furious. There was a terrible row and Chris walked out. It was after that when we discovered the full extent of Chris's theft from the business.'

'So that's why you became the new owner?'

'That's right. When Chris was no longer capable of helping my father, he asked me if I would join the business. I couldn't refuse, so at first I helped at weekends, but then I realised that wasn't enough, so I gave up my lectureship and returned to Farwell.

What I hadn't expected was to become the owner so soon. My dad had told us that he intended to work until he was seventy-five. We'd believed him because he'd always been so fit. Then, one day my mother . . . found him . . . ' Paul paused.

'Don't upset yourself. You've told me enough,' Emma said. She wished she could take his pain away.

'No. Let me finish. I need to get it off my chest. You're the first person I've spoken to about all this. I've kept it bottled up inside for so long.'

'Carry on, if it helps.' Emma felt privileged that Paul felt he could confide in her at last.

'My father had died instantly of a massive heart attack. My mother was hysterical. She blamed Chris and the stress he put on us all, but of course we will never know if that was really the cause.'

'Was Chris able to come to your father's funeral?'

'Yes, they let him out for a few hours.'

'Have you . . . have you visited him in prison?'

'Yes, I go regularly once a month, but it's not easy.'

'I'm sure it isn't.'

'Chris seems genuinely sorry for what happened. I'm hoping he's learnt his lesson, but you never know with gamblers. Once temptation comes along, it's so hard not to give in.'

'What will he do when he comes out of prison?'

'Probably help me, but we'll have to see how it goes.'

'Oh Paul, what a sad story! It makes my problems seem insignificant compared with yours.' She took hold of his hand.

'I'm sorry, Emma, if I've upset you, but I thought it was time to tell you the truth.'

'I'm glad you did.' She squeezed his hand.

'And I think it's time we went home,' Paul remarked, looking at his watch. 'I wonder if it's still raining.'

He called the waitress across. She informed them that it was beginning to clear up. 'You'd better leave now, before it starts to rain again,' she told them.

Soon they were driving back to Emma's flat. They were both quiet, thinking of all that had been said during the evening. Before she got out of the car, Paul kissed her passionately. 'Thank you for being such a good listener,' he whispered.

'Thank you for telling me everything,' she replied, kissing him back.

Then suddenly, unexpectedly, as if he'd just remembered something, he pulled away and asked, 'Now Emma, do you still want to be involved with me?'

15

That night, Emma mulled over the events of the evening, especially Paul's question to her. Did she still want to be involved with him? Of course she did. How could he not know that? He'd asked this, just when she thought he'd trusted her at last. She'd tried so hard to reassure him that now he'd told her everything, she wanted even more to be with him, but it seemed that he still wasn't ready to accept her assurances. She would have to work much harder at convincing him, she decided, but the problem was, how could she do this?

★   ★   ★

There were four weeks left before the concert when they would premiere John Grant's new 'Rhapsody in C Minor'. Everyone was looking forward to it, wanting it to be a great success. The orchestra worked very hard and Paul coaxed them all to give their best.

During this time, Emma and Paul spent as much time together as was possible, considering they were both such busy people. They tried very hard to keep it to themselves, not wanting to give the other members of the orchestra cause for speculation.

Emma made further visits to Paul's house and continued to get on well with his mother and daughter.

One evening at the rehearsal, Samantha informed everyone that she had received another letter and telephone call from Nick Brown. She looked very pleased with herself and life in general. Recently she'd often spent time chatting with Paul, but she hadn't tried to monopolise him and Emma no longer felt threatened by her.

Paul then announced, 'I'm delighted to tell you all that after a lot of persuasion on my part, Samantha has agreed to play the solo violin in

Vaughan Williams' 'Lark Ascending,' which we will be performing at our summer concert.'

Everyone clapped and several members patted her on the back. Emma was surprised to see Samantha blush prettily, and thought how radiant she looked.

Emma still felt amazed that Paul had singled her out for his attentions, when he could have had someone as dazzling as Samantha. Then she remembered he had told her that Sam was too much like his ex-wife.

Paul also informed the orchestra that Nick would be coming back to England in the summer to be the piano soloist at the same concert. Samantha couldn't stop beaming and Emma felt no twinges or pangs of regret when Nick's name was mentioned, being now completely overwhelmed by her feelings for Paul.

Her mother rang up one evening and at last Emma felt able to confide in her about Paul. 'We'd love to meet him, dear,' she said excitedly, 'and I know

Gran will be thrilled, too, when she hears that you have a serious boyfriend at last.'

It felt strange to hear Paul described as her boyfriend, Emma thought, but she rather liked it. 'Perhaps at half term,' she replied, 'if Paul can get away from the bookstore. He wants to meet you and Gran. He's heard so much about you all. Or you could come to our next concert?'

'No. We'll wait till you can bring Paul to see us, as Gran is going to stay here until she's fully recovered.'

Now that Paul and Emma were seeing each other on a regular basis, they were more certain of each other's feelings and their frequent silly arguments became a thing of the past. Emma had learnt to control her tongue and everything was going smoothly between them.

About a week before the concert, Paul was looking very cheerful when he met Emma. 'Do you think you could come over to my house tomorrow evening to keep me company, while my mother goes out?' he asked.

'I'd like that,' Emma replied.

'My mother's going on a date!' he laughed.

'Good for her.' Emma smiled.

'John Grant's taking her out for a meal.'

'Ooh, that's really lovely. I do hope they enjoy themselves.'

'I'm sure they will. My mother's fussing around about what to wear. You'd think she was a young girl! I've never seen anything like it,' Paul said in mock exasperation.

'You haven't seen me fussing around about what to wear when I go out with you,' Emma laughed.

'Not yet,' he answered, and Emma blushed.

★   ★   ★

At the final rehearsal before the concert, Paul announced that he had arranged to make a recording of John's new composition. 'I'm sure it's going to prove a very popular work,' he told them.

John was looking very happy that evening. Emma had found out from Paul that his mother and John had both enjoyed their date. 'I think we have a budding romance there.' He smiled. 'She deserves some happiness after the tough time she has had recently.'

Paul informed Emma that his mother was coming to the concert. She'd asked a neighbour to take care of Fleur, but the little girl was not pleased about it. The next time she saw Emma she asked, 'Why can't I come?'

'It's not suitable for children,' she replied.

'You'd only be bored,' her father added.

'No, I wouldn't. Please let me come, Daddy. You let me come at Christmas.'

'This is different. You'll be much better off at home, so no more arguing.'

Emma felt quite sorry for Fleur, so she promised to take her out one evening after school.

'You spoil my daughter,' Paul had said, giving Emma a hug, but she knew that he didn't mind.

★ ★ ★

The day of the concert finally arrived. Everyone was very nervous, but also excited, especially John.

'Supposing the audience don't like my rhapsody?' he kept saying.

'Stop worrying. They'll love it,' Bill assured him. 'It's sensational.'

'Yes, it's great,' everyone told him.

The concert was an enormous success, from the opening bars of their first work to the final chords of the 'Farwell Rhapsody'. It made a fitting climax to the evening. Several people asked if the composition could be repeated at a future concert, as they wanted to hear it again. Paul promised that they would consider this and told them that later in the year, they would be able to buy a recording. They were having a professional CD made of it.

The audience clapped and cheered so much that John had to take several bows. A reporter was there from the local newspaper and he promised to give the work an excellent review.

Afterwards, the members of the orchestra congregated in the other hall to have a celebration party. Emma remembered the last one, and how she'd been dreading it because Nick was going to be there. Her relationship with Paul had been non-existent then. Now it was so different. Emma couldn't believe how lucky she was. When they were alone together, Paul was a changed man with her, always attentive and charming, although he still took care not to single her out too much when they were in company. This suited Emma, as she didn't want to give anyone cause for gossip. However, Paul hadn't yet told her that he loved her, so she had been reticent in revealing her feelings to him. She enjoyed being with him and he seemed to feel the same way, so that was enough for now, she thought.

Everyone was having a good time at the party, dancing, talking, eating and drinking. John and Paul were very much in demand, and Emma felt pleased for them both, that the concert had gone so well.

'This has been a wonderful evening,' Colin remarked when he danced with Emma. 'John's so talented and Paul's turned out to be a better conductor than I expected. In fact he's been much more human and approachable recently. Have you noticed? Silly question . . . I'm sure you have. Must be a woman who's brought that about. I'm quite sure it's not Samantha. She seems more interested in Nick Brown these days. So I guess that woman's you. Am I right, Emma? You never did answer my question when I asked if you and Paul were going out together. What's your answer?'

'Yes, John is really clever,' Emma replied, ignoring Colin's questions about Paul. 'I'm so glad I joined the orchestra, aren't you?'

'Definitely. Emma. How about you and I going out to celebrate that fact one evening?' he asked, 'if you're not going out with Paul of course. You've still avoided answering my question.'

'Oh Colin, I think it's better if we don't. I thought I'd explained all that to you a long time ago.'

'I know what you said, but I thought there was no harm in asking. You know how I feel about you. I was hoping you might have changed your mind. Going out together could have been fun.'

'But it's all futile, Colin. Forget me. Find someone else.'

'That sounds so final. Okay, I give up. I can't compete with Paul. Your refusal to answer my question has confirmed my worst fears. I just hope you won't regret it, Emma.'

To Emma's relief, the dance finished and they walked back to their places.

'Come on, you two,' Anthea interrupted. 'It's time we got ourselves something to eat. Otherwise all the best things will be gone.'

'Yes, I am rather hungry,' Emma replied, flashing a look of gratitude to Anthea, who smiled broadly.

They all sat together for a while, enjoying both the food and the companionship. Emma looked around and noticed Paul dancing with Samantha. They were chatting and smiling, but she felt no pangs of jealousy. She hoped that Paul had felt the same way when she'd danced with Colin. Then Bill asked Anthea to dance and one of the middle-aged ladies from the orchestra whisked Colin off.

Emma went to the bar to get another drink, when Paul came up and whispered in her ear, 'Can we slip away for a little while? It's a lovely night. How about a short walk? We won't stay out long. No one will miss us.'

'Are you sure? You are the conductor after all. Won't people expect you to be around?' Emma wanted to go with Paul, but felt that it might be embarrassing if it was noted that they had gone off together.

'It's John's night. He's the centre of attention. It won't hurt if we're missing for a while. Come on, Emma.'

'All right,' she replied breathlessly, looking round the hall. Paul was right, no one was looking at them. They were all too busy eating, drinking, dancing or just sitting in a group around John, chatting. They collected their coats from the cloakroom and Paul took her hand as they ambled through the car park towards the river. A myriad of stars was shining down on them. 'It's a perfect evening,' Emma breathed, feeling so happy.

They crossed the bridge over the river and then stopped to look back at the lights of Farwell town, which were twinkling brightly. Paul put his arms around Emma, gave her a long, lingering kiss as she felt herself melt into his embrace.

Suddenly he stopped, pulled away and said, 'There's something else I have to tell you.'

'You have something else to tell me?' Emma repeated worriedly. 'I thought we'd finished all our confessions.' *Now what is Paul going to say?* she wondered.

They walked along the towpath, arms entwined. 'After my . . . my divorce,' Paul started hesitantly, 'I vowed I would never fall in love again. I didn't want to go through all that pain a second time.'

'That's just what I said after Nick ran off with Chelsea,' Emma interrupted.

'Let me go on, please,' Paul continued. 'Then I joined Farwell Orchestra and immediately met you and all my previous ideas went out of the window. I was attracted to you from the very first moment I saw you in the car park, when you gave me such an indignant look after we bumped into each other. I didn't want to feel that way, and get involved again, so I tried very hard to resist you. That's why I was so difficult to get on with, but in the end I couldn't help myself. I felt I had to ask you out, but nothing went according to plan on that date, so I didn't dare suggest another in case you rejected me.'

'Oh Paul, I never guessed any of this.'

'I was so miserable,' Paul continued. 'I couldn't get you out of my system. Then I saw you with Colin and I was eaten up with jealousy. I thought you were interested in him and had just been leading me on. I tried to convince myself that you were like my ex-wife, and that I'd be better off without you. It didn't work. I knew then that I was a hopeless case, completely and irreversibly in love with you, but I didn't know what to do about it. You seemed so distant and cold towards me.'

'But, Paul — ' Emma started to speak.

'No. Please let me finish. I need to say this. When I missed some of our rehearsals because Fleur was ill in hospital, and everyone discovered that I had a daughter, I saw another side to you. Others were ready to condemn me, believing the worst, but you stood by me, even though I hadn't told you the truth. I began to hope once more that I might have a chance with you, until . . . until we had that wretched argument about Nick. Then I feared that everything was finally over.'

'So did I,' Emma said.

'Yes. It was all so stupid. I knew by then that you were not like my wife and I should have trusted you. I'm so sorry for all the unkind things I said. I suppose I was testing you to see what you'd do. But underneath I've always known that you were the girl I wanted, right from that first meeting when you shouted at me. But you always seemed more interested in everyone else. I began to realise that I would have to fight the opposition if I hoped to get anywhere with you.'

'There was no opposition, Paul. It was you I wanted all the time. We've been so silly, having all those futile arguments and . . . '

Emma couldn't continue. Paul stopped walking, took her in his arms and kissed her long and passionately. Then he looked into her eyes and murmured the words she'd wanted to hear for so long. 'I love you, Emma. Will you marry me?'

'Yes, Paul, I will, and I love you too.' She could hardly believe this was happening.

'Oh, Emma.' He kissed her again. Than he released her and they continued walking. 'Shall we have a service of blessing in Farwell Parish Church after the ceremony at the Registry Office Service?' he asked. 'And John could play the organ for us.'

'You've got it all planned out,' Emma laughed. 'Yes, that would be wonderful.'

'I've thought of nothing else for the past few weeks since we've been going out together, but I didn't know what your reaction would be and I was waiting for the right moment to say all this. Tonight seemed a good idea, after the great success of the concert. Arranging our wedding makes it just perfect. I can't believe how fortunate I am, Emma, in getting a second chance like this.'

'Not half as lucky as I am. All my dreams have come true.' She paused. 'But Paul, there's someone else to consider. Fleur. What will she think about this?'

'She'll be delighted. She loves you, too. She needs the influence of a young woman in her life. My mother's very good with her but she is a grandmother figure.'

'So you just want me as a mother substitute. Is that what you're after?' Emma asked quickly.

'No. Don't say that.' Paul was looking concerned.

'I was teasing,' She grinned.

Paul gave a relieved smile and they hugged and kissed again, until he said, 'I think we'd better go back to the party. I think they might be missing us now. We have been rather a long time.'

'They'll be wondering what's going on.'

'Well, now seems like a good time to tell them. What do you say, Emma? Shall I let them know?'

'Oh yes, Paul. And afterwards I must ring up my parents. They'll be thrilled. Two engagements in a few months!'

'Of course. You told me your brother got engaged recently. Your mum and dad will be excited. I think my mother will be delighted too, and Fleur.'

They returned to the hall, still clasping hands, and were immediately spotted by Bill as they entered. 'Aha, what's going on here?' he chortled. 'Where have you two been, and more to the point what have you been up to?'

'Bill!' Anthea exclaimed crossly. 'Don't be so nosy. Take no notice of him,' she said to Paul and Emma. 'He speaks before he thinks.'

'Okay, I'll say no more.' Bill grinned, going to the bar and grabbing himself another drink.

'That's all right. We've something to tell you all in a few minutes but first I must go and have a word with John. I'll be back soon,' Paul said, squeezing Emma's hand.

'If that means what I think it does,

I'm so pleased for you both,' Anthea replied, giving Emma a hug.

'How did you know?' Emma whispered. 'I thought we'd managed to keep it quiet.'

'I just had a feeling about it. I noticed the way you looked at each other.'

I suppose some of the others might have guessed too, Emma thought, watching Colin, who was chatting to Samantha. *I wonder what their reaction will be to our news?*

'What is going on?' Bill muttered as he returned from the bar. 'Several people seem to think that . . . '

'Wait and see,' Anthea interrupted, putting her finger on her lips. 'Now, sit here and behave yourself.'

'You're a very bossy woman,' he groaned, slumping down beside her.

Emma sat watching as Paul beckoned to a couple of the percussion players, who immediately started handing round glasses, while another member poured champagne into them. When they'd finished, Paul banged on the table for silence.

'We've had a wonderful and successful evening. Thank you for all your hard work and dedication to the orchestra. I think we should drink a toast to John and his 'Farwell Rhapsody'.'

'You mean, his *perfect* rhapsody,' Bill added.

'Sorry,' Paul amended. 'Please raise your glasses to John and his perfect rhapsody.'

'To John' echoed round the hall, as he bowed and smiled. Paul's mother patted him on the back and John took her hand and kissed it as everyone cheered.

'Before you all leave, there's one more thing I must do,' Paul said, beckoning to Emma.

'What's that?' Bill asked, winking at Anthea. 'Tell us, Paul. Put us out of our misery.'

Emma flushed with happiness, walked slowly over to Paul, and he put his arm around her as she smiled shyly. 'I just want you all to know that I am the luckiest man in the world because Emma has consented to be my wife.'

Everyone cheered as Paul kissed Emma. His mother shrieked with joy and rushed over to them, hugging them both in turn. 'You make a lovely couple. Fleur will be over the moon. If only your father could have been here to see this,' she added wistfully. 'Still, this is no time to be mournful. We must look to the future. Isn't that right, John?'

'It certainly is. Congratulations, Emma and Paul.' He beamed. 'I'm sure you'll be very happy. This has been some evening!'

'Well done, you two,' Bill joined in. 'Now I know what all the whispering was about.'

Anthea hugged the young couple and said, 'I guessed this was going to happen.'

'Nothing escapes you,' Bill answered proudly, giving Anthea a squeeze.

In her daze of happiness, Emma observed that even Samantha and Colin were cheering. She must have completely got over her infatuation with Paul, Emma thought, feeling glad. She wanted everyone else to be as contented as she was, but what about Colin? How was he feeling?

When he saw Emma looking at him, Colin smiled and came over to them. He shook Paul's hand and gave Emma a kiss on her forehead. 'I won't pester you any more,' he whispered. 'I accept defeat.' Then aloud he said, 'I'd like to offer you both my congratulations.'

'Thank you. I hope that one day you'll be as happy as we are,' Paul answered graciously.

Bill signalled for quiet. 'I'd like to propose a toast, to Emma and Paul. May their life together be like a perfect rhapsody.'

Everyone laughed and continued cheering.

THE END

We do hope that you have enjoyed reading this large print book.

Did you know that all of our titles are available for purchase?

We publish a wide range of high quality large print books including:
Romances, Mysteries, Classics
General Fiction
Non Fiction and Westerns

Special interest titles available in large print are:
The Little Oxford Dictionary
Music Book, Song Book
Hymn Book, Service Book

Also available from us courtesy of Oxford University Press:
Young Readers' Dictionary
(large print edition)
Young Readers' Thesaurus
(large print edition)

For further information or a free brochure, please contact us at:
Ulverscroft Large Print Books Ltd.,
The Green, Bradgate Road, Anstey,
Leicester, LE7 7FU, England.
Tel: (00 44) 0116 236 4325
Fax: (00 44) 0116 234 0205

Other titles in the
Linford Romance Library:

NONE BUT HE

Patricia Robins

When Mandy's boyfriend dies in a motorbike accident, she is left alone with a young child and little money. So when her son's uncle Jon offers her a job as his receptionist — as well as a home with himself and his beautiful but spoilt wife, Gillian — she gratefully accepts. But Mandy soon becomes aware of Jon's unhappiness, as well as her own growing love for him. Perhaps if she accepts the attentions of Mike Sinclair, an attractive Irish bachelor, it will help her to keep her true feelings hidden . . .

THE GHOST OF CHRISTMAS PAST

Sally Quilford

When a man is found dead in macabre circumstances, reverend's daughter Elizabeth Dearheart is thrown into a mystery. Who is the enigmatic Liam Doubleday, and what secret does he keep? Who is the mysterious Lucinda that seems to have haunted the dead man? As Christmas approaches, and Elizabeth begins to fall deeply in love, dark truths come to light and Liam's life hangs in the balance. Elizabeth must uncover the truth before losing him forever . . .

HEALING THE HEART

Charlotte McFall

Tammy Morgan has lost her man, her best friend and very nearly her own life in a short space of time. Struggling to get back on track, and raising her son Toby alone, she makes sure Toby has everything he wants — except a daddy. Then Tammy's ex, Jason Rivera, returns home from Afghanistan, a changed man. Have the mental and physical scars of both their lives healed enough to enable them to rekindle the love they once had for each other?

FIT FOR LOVE

Margaret Mounsdon

Stacey and her stepbrother, Ben, are shocked when Ben's father, Max, announces he is to retire and hand over the reins of his business to Rafe Stocker — a relative stranger to the two siblings. Rafe appoints Stacey as his second-in-command, an offer she feels an obligation to accept, if only to prove that there is room for women in business — something Max has never believed in. But how does Max know the mysterious Rafe, and why did he choose him to run the business? Stacey is determined to find out . . .

SPECIAL MESSAGE TO READERS

THE ULVERSCROFT FOUNDATION
(registered UK charity number 264873)
was established in 1972 to provide funds for research, diagnosis and treatment of eye diseases. Examples of major projects funded by the Ulverscroft Foundation are:-

- The Children's Eye Unit at Moorfields Eye Hospital, London
- The Ulverscroft Children's Eye Unit at Great Ormond Street Hospital for Sick Children
- Funding research into eye diseases and treatment at the Department of Ophthalmology, University of Leicester
- The Ulverscroft Vision Research Group, Institute of Child Health
- Twin operating theatres at the Western Ophthalmic Hospital, London
- The Chair of Ophthalmology at the Royal Australian College of Ophthalmologists

You can help further the work of the Foundation by making a donation or leaving a legacy. Every contribution is gratefully received. If you would like to help support the Foundation or require further information, please contact:

**THE ULVERSCROFT FOUNDATION
The Green, Bradgate Road, Anstey
Leicester LE7 7FU, England
Tel: (0116) 236 4325**

website: www.foundation.ulverscroft.com